THE TRANSFORMATIVE
POWER OF LOVE

THE TRANSFORMATIVE
POWER OF LOVE

MICHAEL H. MITIAS

RESOURCE *Publications* · Eugene, Oregon

Resource Publications
An Imprint of Wipf and Stock Publishers
199 W. 8th Ave., Suite 3
Eugene, OR 97401

www.wipfandstock.com

PAPERBACK ISBN: 978-1-7252-6286-7
HARDCOVER ISBN: 978-1-7252-6285-0
EBOOK ISBN: 978-1-7252-6287-4

Manufactured in the U.S.A.   02/07/20

For Ron Yarbrough
In memory of Jean Yarbrough

In love and esteem

Contents

ONE

Funeral of Mikhail Mitya

"THANK GOD, HE IS finally dead!" Nick Mitya snarled with an unmistakable display of disgust as he scrutinized the corpse that was covered with large chunks of ice in a make-shift coffin.

"You should not talk this way! The man is dead." This from his cousin Nadim, who had just finished saying a prayer of intermission for the soul of his dead uncle, Mikhail Mitya. "He is your uncle."

"I hope his soul sizzles in the fires of hell!" Sparks of spite exploded from Nick's eyes. "Look at this cursed face! Even a child can read the story of his crimes on his forehead."

"Stop talking this way!" Nadim implored, this time emphatically. "He might still hear you, Nick. People say that the soul of a dead man does not leave him until he is buried. Be careful—"

"But, I am careful." Nick snapped. "I wish he hears me, and I wish he knows how much I loathe him. I just hope that my wish rings clearly in his ears when he roasts in the fires of hell!"

"This is not the way to say good-bye to your Uncle. You should say a prayer!"

"Prayer?" Nick ejaculated with a barely audible chuckle and added, "My wish is my prayer. This is the only prayer he deserves. He paused for a moment and continued, "This is the only prayer he needs!"

"Do not be vengeful!"

"Vengeful?" Nick blurted.

"Lower your voice! The room is full of people. They may hear you!"

1

"Let –" Nick could not complete his sentence. One of the mourners, a young lady, dressed in black, tapped his right shoulder softly. She was carrying a brass tray covered with demitasse cups of Syrian coffee.

"Would you like a cup of coffee, Uncle Nick, and you too, Uncle Nadim?" She inquired and then timidly added in a whisper, "The neighbors and some of the Hanano Street merchants began to drift in. They would like to take a look at my grandfather before they leave. I did not mean to interrupt your prayer, Uncle Nick. I just wanted you to know what is going on."

"Oh, no, Jeanette," Nick said, interrupting his niece, "I have already said my prayer and—" He hesitated a little, then continued with a shade of sarcasm tingeing his voice, "May he enjoy an eternal life of—" He stopped, grinned derisively and continued, "You know what I mean! I only hope that God heard me. May he grant Uncle Mikhail my wish!"

Although Jeanette did not hear the exchange between the two cousins, she found her Uncle's response cryptic, if not oracular. She felt an urge to ask for a clarification of his meaning, but her immediate duties were to attend to the other mourners.

The Mitya house sat on four groined vaults, two on the southern side, one on the eastern side, and the fourth on the northern side. The northern vault was used as a kitchen. One of its corners functioned as a kitchenette. The eastern vault served as a living room and was separated from the southern vault by a corridor that connected the entrance with the courtyard. When he was alive, Mikhail occupied one of the southern vaults, and his wife, Rachel, occupied the other. Upon Mikhail's death, his room was transformed into a funeral chamber, while the living room performed double duty as a reception space for the women mourners.

The reception room was lined with three rows of chairs, one against each wall. The women mourners were dressed in black. Almost all of them had covered their hair with a black veil. They did not wear any make-up, not even rouge. "Death was supposed to be a moment of truth, and truth should not be covered!" This is what the priest said. But although they were clad in black, the expressions on their faces were grim, as if doomsday was around the corner, each carried a visible white handkerchief in their right hand. They were ever prepared to shed tears for the permanent departure of dear Mikhail, patriarch of the family! A professional wailer, also dressed in black, sat in the corner of the room. She chanted the most emotional, most grief-stricken songs you can imagine. They were so melancholy, so moving, so contagious, even a stranger who listened to them attentively would become a momentary mourner. The songs, which she chanted in a droopy, languishing voice, were pleas to the family ancestors in another world to welcome one of their sons, Mikhail, into their holy presence, as well as to assure them that the Mitya family here on earth was thriving.

The wailing was an occasion to convey packages of love and yearning from the living friends and family members to those already dead! The wailer frequently asked the mourners to join her in wailing and repeat, especially emotional refrains. "Wail with me, dear sisters," she would chant in a sad voice. "Oh, wail with me for the permanent departure of dear Mikhail. Oh, Mariana, mother of the Mityas, your descendants, welcome your great-grandson, Mikhail!" Once in a while, one of the mourners would interrupt the wailer and ask her to wail for her dead husband, brother, or son. Wailing sessions were used as reminders that life is short and that eternal life is an extension of the present life.

The Mitya family was a patriarchal family *pur excellence*: men and women displayed radically different behavior. Men were men and behaved like men, while women were women and behaved like women. Each one of the sexes understood the nature of their gender identity, accepted it, and in some cases, were proud of it. Men were in charge of the external affairs of the family, particularly the means of survival; women were in charge of its internal affairs, such as the kitchen and raising the children. Men acted as the guardians of the family; women were guardians of its traditions and values. Men stood on the ground of law and justice; women stood on the ground of love and forgiveness. Men were the stronger sex; women were the weaker sex. Men were rational beings; women were emotional beings. When the patriarch of the family spoke, everyone listened, even when his speech was wrong, foolish, or stupid. Patriarchy was not invented by the Mitya family or any other family; it was ordained by God The Father. This ordinance was stated in the bible. Patriarchy was an established way of life. Questioning it, especially in the Mitya family, was like challenging the laws of nature.

The male mourners mingled in the courtyard. They formed small groups—neighbors with neighbors, friends with friends, merchants with merchants, and churchgoers with churchgoers. Unlike the women who were dressed in black, the men wore either a black band on their forearm or a black ribbon on the lapel of their jacket, and unlike the women, whose task it was to lament the death of the oldest member of the family and act as mediators between the living and the dead, the men discussed the crucial matters and problems of life: business, politics, scandals of the day, crime, personal adventures, and the weather. The question of death, the immortality of the soul, justice, the meaning of human life, beauty, whether Mikhail was going to heaven or hell, or even whether heaven and hell existed, was the farthest thing from their minds. They were real men. Real men are sons of the earth! They are familiar with the dynamics of human nature and the secret of human life. They also know that real life is the only school where they can learn the nature and meaning of human life and destiny. They send their children to academic schools not to learn the purpose of a good life or the art of human living but the *art of money-making*. Money, not knowledge, is power—the real power in this world. It is the key to security, peace, pleasure, and prosperity. What more should we expect from life? Books, art, science, philosophy, even the sermons of the priest, are mere words—empty words. They are essential to dreamers, idlers, and flunkies but not to real people. Real people are adept at struggling, making money, and protecting their families. They know how to survive in a world governed by the laws of the jungle.

These laws govern the various activities of human life on the ground of reality. What about the doctrines of the scientist, the philosopher, the social reformer, and the theologian? For the Mitya men, they are social ornaments—beautiful ideals, but they are not the governing laws of actual life at the individual, economic, and political levels. These laws are masks, pretty garments people wear in the social market. They are a means to an end, and the end is survival. The instinct of survival is the strongest in human nature; it underlies the decisions and actions of the philosopher, the priest, the scientist, the social reformer, and the politician. Morsels of pleasure now and then are the greatest delight for the majority of people. "Do you think," Nick once said, "that your priest, philosopher, or social reformer is willing to die, or even go to prison, for the sake of your moral and rational laws? They value them, defend them, treasure them, and live according to their principles only to the extent of ensuring their survival. These individuals abandon such laws, and they rationalize this abandonment convincingly, but in fact, spuriously, the moment their life is threatened. The secret agents in the various countries of the world who torture spies, criminals, and traitors to extol some information from them, know the validity of the laws of nature more than the philosopher, the scientist, the social reformer, or the priest!" The Mitya men were the secret agents of human nature and human life.

A stranger, who was weaving his way through the different aggregations of the mourners, suddenly stopped next to three members of the Mitya family. They were engaged in a heated conversation about what seemed to be a serious problem. The stranger's sudden appearance, which might be viewed as an intrusion or perhaps a request to join them, froze their conversation in mid-sentence. Six eyes were instantly directed at him. He met their gazes with a friendly smile and a gentle nod as if to say, "Good morning!" or "Peace be upon you!" The three men were lost to a long moment of confused silence. "Good morning!" Nadim jubilated after extricating himself from the indolence of the moment. However, his eyes remained glued to the eyes of the stranger.

"Good morning!" The stranger returned. "Please, allow me to introduce myself," he continued, "I am Johannes Mitya—"

"Johannes Mitya?" Nadim exclaimed impulsively, accenting the family name. The mere mention of his name ignited a storm of apprehension, curiosity, and doubt in the three cousins. Jirji, the youngest, was particularly curious about the identity of the stranger. "Is he a distant relative?" he thought. "Impossible, because I know every member of the family. Are there other Mitya families? I wonder!" Those questions coursed through his mind, but he could not dwell on them.

"Did you say Johannes Mitya?" Jirji asked aloud this time.

"Yes, my full name is Johannes Mitya. Mikhail Mitya, the man who lies dead in the coffin in the vault behind you, is my grand uncle." Baffled, the three cousins looked at each other and then back at the stranger.

"Are you sure that the dead man is your grand uncle?" Nick intervened with a suppressed chuckle of disbelief, his eyes never leaving the face of the stranger. "Is he an imposter?" he thought in the privacy of his mind. "What does he want? Does he expect some kind of inheritance or favor from the family?" Neither Nadim nor Jirji interrupted Nick's interrogation.

"I am as sure as you are of your own existence." Dumbfounded, the three cousins glanced at each other again and cautiously returned their collective gaze to the stranger. However, the young man was not deterred by their bafflement and skepticism. On the contrary, he responded with a cordial, and one can say, compassionate look at Nick. A second later, he presented the same countenance to the other cousins. In such moments, ignorance of the other, the mysterious other, is frequently a source of fear, suspicion, and sometimes of hostility. Compassion, self-composure, and an attitude that inspires trust do not only shatter the wall that exists between the persons who face each other for the first time, it also creates a bridge of communication, of acceptance, and sometimes of mutual understanding.

"But why don't we know you?" Nick asked. "I think that no one in the Mitya family here in Latakia either knows about or ever heard of you."

"Yes," the stranger responded, "you have not heard of me because I have not been here for a long time—"

"How long?" Nick queried. Curiosity was mounting in his mind, accelerating with each passing moment!

"About three months."

"Where did you live before coming to Latakia?" Nick asked.

"Germany."

"Germany?" Nick exclaimed. His simmering curiosity ignited that of his cousins. Nick, who could not control himself any longer, giggled disdainfull escaping his lips. When the stranger noticed that this reaction was mirrored by the other cousins, he simply smiled and resorted to silence. In fact, Johannes had expected this kind of response. It was natural for them or anyone to react this way. When you are innocent, and when you are honest, you do not show any signs of fear, guilt, doubt, or hesitation. If you do, you intensify the uncertainty and fear of others. The actions of an innocent person flow spontaneously, irresistibly, from their heart. They stand their ground with confidence, self-confidence, and mental lucidity.

"As far as I know," Nick continued, "there are no Mitya families in Swaydieh anymore. All of them migrated to Latakia during the Second World War. What you say, friend, is puzzling, to say the least. But suppose you are a Mitya, how do you know about our uncle and particularly about his death?"

"Let me first assure you that I am a true Mitya and that I am indeed your cousin. Your parents, and perhaps the oldest living member of the family in Latakia, did not give you an accurate account of your family tree. I am now convinced that you are not well informed about the history of the Mitya clan that descends from the patriarch Abraham. Our patriarch did not have five, but ten sons and one daughter. Only six sons survived. Hanania Sr., my grandfather, was the youngest, and frequently talked about his brother Mikhail, your uncle, and mine, who died two days ago. Mikhail was his favorite brother. He admired him immensely."

"Admired him immensely?" Nick interjected angrily.

"Yes, he thought that Mikhail was brilliant, handsome, and brave. He emphasized that he was honest and loyal to his friends and every member of the family—"

"Oh, my God!" Nick mumbled imprudently. Even though the mumble was rather faint, the stranger heard it but chose to ignore it.

"I admit that my grandfather did not know about the life or whereabouts of his brothers and their children because he immigrated to Germany in 1890, but—"

"Ah, yes." Nick interrupted the stranger again, but this time with more confidence. "How could he know about them if he lived in Germany practically all his life? Did he correspond with them? No, because someone would have mentioned his letters. Did he visit them? No, because if he did, or if any of his brothers visited him, we would certainly know about it. I am not sure that you are a Mitya, and even if you were, you must be a member of a German Mitya family, not ours! I am not even sure why you are here at this funeral."

"Don't be hasty, Nick. Let the man answer your questions first." Jirji interrupted him and gently, imperceptibly, stepped on his cousin's foot as if to insist that he should allow the stranger to tell his story. Although reluctantly, Nick resorted to silence with disbelief plain in his eyes.

"You see, Nick, my grandfather did not know how to read and write German, Turkish, or Arabic. He worked in a textile factory, and his employer considered him an excellent silk weaver. My grandfather learned the craft of silk-weaving when he was a teenager in Antioch. He was highly respected for his efficiency and dedication to his work, family, and church. He made sure that every one of his children attends university since he valued education more than anything in his life. And, to tell the truth, his children, and now his grandchildren, are highly educated and successful young men and women. They are proud of their grandfather and of the cultural legacy he left them—"

This narrative was interrupted by the unexpected appearance of Jeannette carrying a tray of coffee cups. "Would you like a cup of coffee, Uncle Nadim?" she asked as she was stealing a glance at the stranger.

"Why don't you serve our guest, first, my dear?" he said and pointed to the stranger. Her hands trembled a little when she moved the brass tray closer to the guest.

"Would you like a cup of coffee?" she asked.

"Yes, I would, Jeannette." He threw a quick look at her and said, "Jeannette—am I correct?" Flabbergasted, the three cousins stared at the stranger with bewildered eyes. "He even knows Jeannette's name!" Nick thought. "Who is he? He must be some kind of spy!" He seems to know a great deal about us—but how much does he really know?" Contrarily, Jirji thought that they should listen to the stranger's entire story before passing judgment on his credibility. Nadim, on the other hand, was unable to form an opinion. The story, indeed the whole situation, was confusing to him.

"Yes, I am Jeannette."

"My uncle Mikhail spoke very highly of you. He was proud of you. He is right—you favor my father, who, in turn, favors his father. I am delighted to meet you." Jeannette's cheeks were instantly aflame, her lips trembling slightly. Although she did not respond to the stranger's remarks, she was confounded, to say the least. She turned her eyes away from him and moved the tray toward Jirji. She was so confused and bewildered that she forgot to serve Nick.

"What about me?" Nick called when she was on her way to the kitchen. "I am not invisible, honey!" Jeannette retraced her steps and served him a cup of coffee. Instead of the rosy radiance of moments ago, her face had visibly paled when she left her uncle.

"What strikes me as baffling, if not weird, is that you came to Latakia without even introducing yourself to your family. If you are a Mitya, you should have paid a visit to one of us, but you did not." Johannes listened to Nick's interrogative retort with a frown on his brow, seemingly deep in thought. What Nick had said was logical. Was the stranger an imposter?

"What you have just said is reasonable," Johannes said. "You are right, I should have come directly to someone in the Mitya family, but the sequence of events that occurred on the ship before we docked in the Latakia harbor after my arrival prevented me from reaching out to the family."

"What kind of events are you speaking of? What you say seems exceedingly farfetched. Do you expect any sane person to believe you?"

"I shall be pleased to answer your question if you promise not to interrupt me."

"Fine," Nick said, "but please make it brief because the priest will arrive for a short liturgy any minute."

"I shall try." Jirji and Nadim were relieved. They, too, were anxious to discover the identity of the young man who seemed to know so much about their family. Frankly, they thought Nick's retort to the stranger was both bold and confrontational, perhaps combative, but they did not have time to intervene since the exchange between Nick and the stranger was already underway.

"That is all I ask," Nick said.

Johannes proceeded with this explanation, "I boarded The Leipzig in Hamburg about four months ago. The trip lasted one month. It stopped in several ports—Rotterdam, Lisbon, Barcelona, Naples, and Piraeus. I met a Syrian student, called Salim Schuman, on the ship. He is from Bouqa, a suburb of Latakia, as you know. He had just graduated from the College of Agriculture at the University Munich with a degree in horticulture. He was on his way to Latakia. He plans to teach at the school of agriculture in Bouqa and is a highly refined human being. I was delighted to meet a young man from Latakia, and he was equally delighted to discover that I was a Mitya and that I was going to Latakia. Salim is highly knowledgeable about the Mitya family, and I gleaned from the many remarks and anecdotes he relayed to me that our family is extensive, almost a clan. Salim emphasized that it is a renowned family, and I quickly discovered that he knew more, much more about our family than he at first divulged. You see, he was a classmate of Uncle Hanania's oldest son, Majdi. Salim went to the University of Munich on a government scholarship, and Majdi went to the U.S. after they graduated from high school. 'We were very close friends,'" Salim elaborated, 'we shared many of our feelings, problems, and aspirations during our high school years. His mother treated me as her son. She made me feel at home every time I visited Majdi. There is no need to tell you how much I know about the Mitya family in Latakia, but I know enough to make me feel proud of it.'"

"The first thing I did when the ship docked in the harbor was to submit our passports to the Immigration authority and then go to the waiting room. Salim's parents were waiting for him. They welcomed their son with hugs, kisses, and tears in their eyes. They were proud of him, and their pride intensified when they discovered that he was cited as an honor student during the graduation ceremony. Salim introduced me to his parents as soon as he was able to extricate himself from their arms and informed them that I was planning to do research in the district of Latakia. They were thrilled to make my acquaintance and happier still to know that I was a Mitya. 'We know your uncles, and we know your grand-uncle, Mikhail,' Salim's father, Nabeel, said as soon as we occupied our seats in the car. You shall stay with us until you find an apartment and get settled in it.'"

"But I do not wish to be a burden—"

"Oh, goodness! You shall never be a burden, not on the Schuman family. My wife, Samia, will be delighted to have you as our honored guest!"

"We left the harbor as soon as our passports and luggage were checked. There was not a dull moment in the car. Samia showered Sami with a barrage of questions. She was anxious to find out as much as possible about the details of his practical life in Germany, not because she was interested in them but because she wanted to know whether he left a girlfriend or perhaps a fiancée behind. 'You will be surprised to know,' she said to Johannes, 'that many young men who go to foreign countries to complete their studies do not, in fact, complete them. They meet a beautiful woman, fall in love, get married, find a mediocre job, and forget about their education and their families. They never come back, not even for a visit. What is sad is that many of these marriages never last! Is this fair to them and to their parents?'"

"But Samia," Nabeel remarked, "Not all men and women are alike," and with a chuckle added, "Salim would not do such a thing!"

"I know," Samia continued, "but—"

At this point in the unexpected exchange, Salim, who was listening to his mother attentively, intervened. This was not the first time Samia had expressed her fears about the possibility of her son getting married to a foreign girl. He assured her, hopefully for the last time, that he was not attached to a German woman or any woman for that matter, and that he was a free man. 'I doubt that I shall be returning to Germany in the foreseeable future, Mother. Besides,' he added, "honestly, Mother, I did not have time to flirt with girls, much less establish a relationship with one. Study and fun are not compatible bedfellows." This response, which shed ample light on Salim's character, elicited a happy smile from Samia. It was clear to Nabeel that his wife would like Salim to marry a young woman from Bouqa.

This lively, yet interesting conversation was interrupted by a commotion that streamed through the entrance of the Mitya residence. The cousins, as well as the guests, turned toward its source. The priest and two deacons were rushing through the hallway to the courtyard. One of the deacons was carrying a bag and the other a rectangular case. Abraham and Hanania, Mikhail's sons, who were expecting him, led the priest to the funeral chamber. The different groups of mourners instantly dispersed and followed the priest. The wailing stopped, and a long line of sad-looking women, who were wiping their eyes with white handkerchiefs, followed the men. "We should continue this conversation!" Nick said.

"We certainly should!" Nadim emphasized.

"Do you have any engagements this evening, Johannes?" Jirji asked.

"No. I intended to return to Bouqa as soon as my grand uncle was buried. The schedule of my daily activities is not finalized yet—"

"Where are you staying?" Jirji asked.

"The Schumans helped me find an apartment near the School of Agriculture. It is small, but it is comfortable and meets my needs adequately. I am now in the process of organizing it, I hope to start working in a few days."

"If you need any kind of assistance now or in the future, please let me or Nadim know. We shall do all we can to make your stay in Latakia as commodious as possible. Do not plan on returning to Bouqa immediately following the burial. My cousins and I would like to share supper with you this evening." Jirji said with a genial smile.

The funeral chamber was crowded, and so was the vault connected to it. The three cousins and the stranger watched the funeral liturgy through the window of the room. One of the deacons, who held the censor, and the other, who held the bible in his right hand, acted as chanters. The coffin was placed in the middle of the chamber. Every few minutes, the priest circled it, sang, and read from the liturgy text. He frequently blessed the dead man with incense and holy water and begged the angels in heaven to keep the evil spirits away from his soul. In the meantime, one of the deacons, who was being prepared for the priesthood, chanted the most solemn, most melancholy, and most doleful songs ever chanted in the Orthodox Church. They were so sad, many of the women were weeping.

When the liturgy was concluded, the priest gave a short sermon on death and dying, as well as the urgent need to live according to the teachings of the holy church. "He gives the same sermon at every funeral. He must have memorized it by heart," Nick mumbled to Nadim. "We need a young priest."

"You mean a more skillful charlatan?" Jirji interjected. "You seem to forget that nowadays the priesthood is a profession, a business, not a way of life. Priests used to be religious models, and are presumably the embodiments of the moral and religious values of the church. But now they are employees of the religious establishment, and like any other business, they are expected to follow certain rules and norms. The church, which is supposed to be the body of Christ, is now the priest's body—without the spirit of Christ. You can say that it is a soul-less body! But what is really sad is that while secular employees are dismissed when they violate the rules and norms of the establishment, priests remain permanent fixtures in the church! No one can remove them from their position. They are appointed for life by the Patriarch. His decisions are consecrated by the Holy Spirit. We are stuck with them until they die."

However, the purpose of the priest's sermon was not to teach or shed any particular light of understanding on the meaning of immortality, happiness, or the virtues of life, but to flatter the family of the deceased. This was an excellent opportunity to extol a substantial benefaction from Abraham and Hanania. As he always did, he sprayed the dead man with flowery words of praise. He described him as a loving and dutiful father and grandfather, who raised one of the finest families in Latakia. "Mikhail," he emphasized, "was a model of honesty, honor, and love. He was devoted to his virtuous wife, Rachel. He was always there whenever any member of the community needed help." These last statements fired an arrow of fury into Nick's mind. It was like a spark of fire igniting a pond of oil into a massive cloud of fire. His throat gurgled, and his shoulders jerked a little. Frankly, he was beside himself. He withdrew from the window and took a deep breath. He could not control himself anymore. He looked sideways as if he was looking for a hiding place or an exit from this ridiculous circus. Jirji, who noticed the sudden transformation in his cousin's complexion and behavior and understood what Nick was experiencing, moved closer to him and whispered in his ear, "This whole charade will be over shortly. Be patient—just a little longer!"

"Did you notice how tears were flowing from Aunt Rachel's eyes like a river when the good clergyman was contaminating the vault with his lies about her husband?" He exclaimed in a somewhat audible voice. Nadim, who did not hear Nick's speech, left the window and joined his cousins. Seeing that Nick was boiling with fury, they simply stood quietly next to him. "This cursed priest, and I think some of the mourners, think that those tears were produced by his florid words. Oh, no, those tears were not produced by the memory of a philanderer, a derelict, a good-for-nothing husband, father, and grandfather, but by a man who neglected his wife and children and spent his life gambling, drinking, and seducing the women of the community with his beautiful blue eyes and alluring smile. This liturgy is a grand show of hypocrisy! Do you think that all the people who are now standing next to his coffin with somber faces know the kind of debaucher he was?" Nick vociferated with angry eyes.

"Oh, Nick, please, compose yourself—" Jirji said in a whisper.

"Compose myself!" Nick interrupted his cousin. "Do you know that some of the Mitya women were his victims? Ask my sister-in-law, Sarah. She knows each of them. Yes, ask some of his victims!"

"I am certain that some of the men here will never forget him. But some of the women will always remember the pleasure he gave them. They are not here to pray for the salvation of your uncle's soul but to condole Abraham and Hanania. Remember: funerals are not for the dead; they are for the living. How can you pray for a person who does not exist anymore?"

"You can because there are heaven and hell." Nick retorted.

"What does heaven or hell have to do with it?

"The immortality of the soul. Undermine belief in the immortality of the soul, and you undermine belief in the existence of heaven and hell. One cannot exist without the other. If you behave according to the teaching of the church, you go to heaven, and if you do not, you go to hell."

"Well, suppose there are heaven and hell. If Uncle Mikhail goes to heaven, he will not need your prayers, and if he does not, he will not need your prayers either."

"What about purgatory? Some Christians believe in it."

"Purgatory does not exist. It is a fiction concocted by some devious Catholic theologians during the middle ages mainly to frighten the sinners and give hope to the faithful. It is a trick practiced by the church to control its flock on the assumption that it could decide who goes to heaven or hell."

Nick darted a curious, and one can say cynical, look at Jirji. Apparently, he never thought about the question of immortality and salvation of the soul. But Jirji continued, "If these people here, indeed all Christians, especially the patriarchs, Popes, bishops, and priests take the idea of heaven and hell seriously, we would not need Sunday schools, monasteries, and schools of theology. If they honestly take the idea of heaven and hell seriously, which implies the existence of the Christian God, they would not dare deviate from the teachings of the church. Who wants to spend an eternity in hell? Who would not do all they can to spend an eternity in heaven, assuming that heaven is a desirable place? So, let me ask you once more, why would you need the whole religious establishment if Christians truly believe that God exists, that Jesus is his son, that his disciples founded the church on the basis of God's word, and that the teaching and action of the church are true to his word?"

"I do not understand much of what you said, Jirji, but it seems to me that your ideas are dangerous."

"But what if it is true? Is the truth dangerous? Yes, it is but only to those who are misguided and those who live in a dark cave of ignorance. Ignorance is the source of evil."

"The ignorant believe that they possess the truth. But what makes me think that your ideas are dangerous is that they seem to make sense. Perhaps this is why the ignorant view them as dangerous. I am afraid that the moment they hear you talk this way, they will ostracize you, shun you like the plague, try to harm you, or even hang you in the public square if they can. The masses are enemies of the truth. Your ideas will definitely scare them, Jirji. I have never heard you talk this way before. Did you express these ideas when you were studying theology at the seminary?"

But Jirji did not answer because the mourners were already leaving the funeral chamber. Abraham and Hanania stood at the entrance of the house and received the condolences of the mourners who were leaving the vault.

As soon as calm returned to the courtyard, Abraham approached his cousins. "I would like you to meet Johannes Mitya," Nick said when he stood next to him.

"Mitya?" Abraham exclaimed, surprised. He fixed Johannes with a look punctuated by curiosity and underscored with a severe frown.

"Johannes is a member of the German branch of the Mitya family," Nick interjected hastily in an attempt to diffuse Abraham's curiosity.

"German branch?" Abraham asked.

"This is what he says." Nick retorted. It was clear to Nadim and Jirji that he, too, was skeptical about their guest's family affiliation. Abraham nodded and cast a second, inquisitive, but friendly look at Johannes. He allowed a soft smile to dance upon his lips. But he was unable to pursue this intriguing conversation because many questions and concerns regarding the funeral were swirling through his mind. He was unable to focus his attention on the guest.

"I am very pleased to meet you, Johannes!" He paused for a second and then added, "I very much appreciate your presence with us on this sad occasion. Now you know where we live. You should visit us as soon as you can," he said and, turning his face toward Nadim, continued, "there is no need for you and Nick to be pallbearers. The young men insisted that they would gladly perform this task. The burial will be at three o'clock. I know you hate burials, but try to attend this one if you can. If you cannot, I shall see you upstairs at the mercy dinner this evening. Most of the family and some friends will be there.

TWO

A Justification of Prayer

WHEN ABRAHAM HAD LEFT, Nadim declared that he would attend the burial, "Even though he does not deserve this honor, I shall bid him good-bye not as an expression of love or respect or even because I shall miss him, but as an expression of celebrating the permanent departure of the black sheep of the family. Our family has always stuck together during good times and bad, and it is vital to respect this tradition. Anyway, I doubt that I shall see him again if what you said about heaven and hell happens to be accurate, Jirji. This is how I feel, and I shall act accordingly. Nick was quick to comment on Nadim's decision.

"I respect your decision, Nadim, and the motive behind it, and I hope you find the burial satisfactory."

"We should always remember," Jirji intervened, "that although he was the black sheep of the family, he was a human being. We should respect him as one! If we do not, we only succeed in reducing ourselves to his low level of humanity."

"You have always thought and acted like a theologian, Jirji. Frankly, I do not understand the way you think and act, but I shall continue to act the way I think and feel." Jirji did not respond to Nick's retort.

"Can I ask you a favor, Nadim?" Nick asked abruptly.

"Of course, you can."

"Would you say a prayer for Uncle Mikhail on my behalf?"

"On your behalf?" Jirji asked incredulously. "How can anyone say a prayer on behalf of somebody else?"

"Are you teasing me, Nick?" Nadim asked.

"No," and, turning to face Jirji, said, "since you know so much about heaven, hell, and God, what do you think? Please, tell us! Can one pray on behalf of somebody else?"

"I do not know much about God, heaven, and hell. However, I know that to be right, at least meaningful, a prayer should originate directly from one's mind and heart, indeed from the totality of their being, otherwise the prayer would be meaningless because it would be reduced to a kind of commodity or an object, one can handle, manipulate, or exchange for a price."

"Are you serious, Jirji? Can you explain?"

"Yes. Prayer is supposed to be a personal encounter between the individual who prays and God. Whether the aim is to thank Him for something, glorify Him for the greatness and magnificence of His creation, or ask Him for some kind of favor, prayer is essentially *confessional in nature*. No one can confess anything on behalf of another human being."

"Do you mean that prayer is a type of dialogue between the individual and God?" Nadim asked.

"No," Jirji said, "because God does not think, feel, and act the way human beings do. Moreover, He has never asked for it or required it of any founder of the major religions of the world. God is not a mega human being. He is indescribable. In short, he is not an object."

"But, then," Nadim asked, "in what sense is prayer an encounter between the individual and God? What kind of encounter is it? How can one stand before a being they cannot describe or know?"

"Although God is not an object of human experience, and although we cannot know Him the way we know ordinary objects, we can experience His presence and know about Him in and through his creation in two basic ways. The first is by contemplating the order of the universe and the amazing fabric of human civilization, while the second is by considering the truth revealed in different religions. This kind of contemplation requires time, concentration, patience, and knowledge of nature and human accomplishments in science, philosophy, and art."

"What do you mean when you speak of knowledge *about* god?"

"We know about God by directly intuiting some of His aspects, radiance, or presence in the world, as well as by inference, that is, by reasoning and reflecting on the infinite complexity of the causal relations which underlie the infinity of the objects that make up the structure of the universe. This twofold assertion is based on the principle of causation: nothing happens, and nothing exists without a cause. Here, we can add that the cause is superior to the effect, for it cannot be the cause of the effect. Accordingly, most, if not all, the time we can infer the cause from its effect and the effect from its cause. For example, we can infer the existence of the light from the existence of the sun and vice versa. We can make this inference because the relation between them is causal: the sun causes the light to exist. If the sun does not exist, the light would not exist. Isn't this what happens when the sun sets behind the horizon?"

"Now, if everything that exists and happens in the human and natural worlds necessarily has a cause, don't you think that it would follow that the totality of existence, which we usually call 'universe,' must have a cause and that the cause must be superior to the universe? Would you agree?"

"I would, but I have a question. In the sun-light example, we know the sun as the cause and the light as an effect because we experience them as such, but in the case of the universe and its cause, we do not experience the direct causal relationship between the universe and its cause? Is there any logical or justifiable reason for saying that the universe necessarily has a cause? It is complicated to say that something exists, even by valid inference, if we cannot experience it. Moreover, is there a reliable basis for any knowledge we infer about the cause of experiencing the universe?"

"First, the universe exists, but it does not have to exist."

"How do we know this?" Nadim asked.

"Every object in the universe and the universe as a whole are in constant motion. This two-fold motion necessarily implies a cause. Moreover, we cannot say that it is self-created, because no object of any kind can come from nothing and because nothing does not exist. Also, if it can come from nothing, it should be able to annihilate itself, which is, so far as we know, inconceivable."

"Can we say its existence is eternal—without a beginning and an end?"

"We can, only if we assume that its cause is not external but internal to it," Jirji said.

"What do you mean?"

"When I say its cause exists internal to it, I mean *it inheres in it*, or, put differently, it is *immanent in it*," Jirji explained.

"Immanent? This term is new to me. Can you explain this type of relation?"

"Let me first say that the kind of act in which God created the universe, and continues to create it, is different from the kind of act in which people create artifacts, for example, a chair or a song. Once the carpenter creates a chair, the chair exists independently of the carpenter. This feature is characteristic of all types of artifactual creation, but it does not apply to the act of divine creation. In fact, we cannot pretend or claim to know any type of divine action because god transcends our capacity of conceiving and knowing. He is, as I've mentioned earlier, indescribable. We are finite; he is infinite in every possible or conceivable dimension of being—"

"But, then, how do we know that he is immanent in the universe? Can you explain the meaning of 'immanence' first?"

"I shall try."

"Thank you, Jirji. I have always believed that you are the thinker of the family!"

"Thinker? You are a very generous person. But I am not a thinker. I am an infant in the art of thinking." Nadim smiled.

"I want you to conjure up in your mind the image of the sun, the same sun that is now standing over our heads. Focus your attention on the relation between the disk and the light that illuminates this courtyard and the entire landscape of Latakia. The sun ceases to exist for us when the light ceases to exist, and the light ceases to exist because the relationship between them is causal. But first, the question we should answer is, *how does the light of the sun exist in our world*? What is its mode of existence? Look at Nick, who stands next to you. He exists in a particular space. His existence is confined to the space he occupies in this courtyard, while the size of the space is the size of his body. This type of existence characterizes the existence of the objects which make up the fabric of the universe—would you agree?"

"Yes."

"Space seems to be a receptacle, a medium in which objects exist. But now let us ask, in what way, or how, does the light that emanates from the sun exist?" Nadim did not answer this question but sought help from Jirji with pleading eyes. "Can we say that it exists on the surface of the earth? No, because the light permeates all the space between the sun and the earth. However, the space is not pure emptiness or nothing, but a reality the way the mountain, the river, and the planets are realities, and, although they are realities, they are also spaces. Yet, even though the space between the earth and the sun exists as a type of reality and not as pure nothing, the light of the sun permeates it—would you agree?

"Yes."

"However, this type of existence is different from that of objects such as mountains and trees. Nevertheless, it is a type of reality. The sun does not exist in the space that separates the sun from the earth but penetrates the totality of its being and exists in this totality simultaneously. It illuminates this space, and in illuminating it, it reveals its nature. It makes it visible; it makes it real to us. Now, this kind, or mode, of existence, Nadim, is called *immanence*. It is an event in which the light of the sun exists simultaneously throughout the space that separates the earth from the sun. The presence of the light in the space is what acquaints us with the existence of the sun. We cannot know what the sun in itself is because it does not exist in the fullness of its being as an immediate object of experience since it is far away from us. In fact, all we know about it, through our vision, is that it is a golden disk. However, we can discover *something about it* by studying the light that emanates from it, as some scientists did during the nineteenth and twentieth centuries. As you see, we know about the existence of the sun, and we know something about it in so far as it is expressed or embodied in its light.

"Now, shift your attention from our sun as the cause of the light, to the cause of the universe. We can liken this cause to the sun with at least one basic difference: the cause of the universe is an infinite source of being, while our sun is a finite cause of being. Just as the light emanates from our sun and exists in the space that separates it from the earth, the universe emanates from God, and God fills the space it occupies. We do not know the limit of this space, but we can say that, as its source, God is immanent in it. This immanence is proportionate to the magnitude and nature of the universe. Therefore, what we know about god is limited to the extent to which it reveals His nature. We cannot know God in himself because He is greater than the universe. His being is richer, infinitely richer than the being of the universe we are talking about."

"In your analogy of the sun, you said that light fills the space which separates the earth from the sun, but in what sense is God immanent in the universe?" Nadim asked.

"He is immanent in the sense that the design and nature of the universe do not only point to His existence but also reveal His nature as the cause and as the administrator of its on-going process of creation."

"Does this mean that God is in the universe or that the universe is a part of God?"

"It is more accurate to say that He is in the universe, in so far as it requires His presence, since His being is, as we have just said, infinitely greater than the being of the universe. Only in this sense is it possible to say that the universe is a part of God. Don't we say that a ray of light forms part of the sun? Moreover, don't we assume that the sun is greater in its being than the being of the ray? Since the being of God is infinitely richer than the being of the universe, He cannot exist in it as an object. The mode of His presence in it is *omnipresence*. This is why it is reasonable to say that he *permeates* the universe the way the light of the sun permeates the space that separates it from the earth. And, since the most prominent dimension of this presence is light, some mystics referred to God metaphorically as The Light, and sometimes as The Sun. God's immanence in the universe is the ontological basis of any cognitive interference we make about his existence or nature. It is easy to see the light of our sun because it is finite and because it directly reaches our eyes, but it is not easy to see the light of the cause of the universe, because it is infinite and because it is not given to our mind or senses as an object. Only a part of His light, the one that permeates the universe that is given to us as presence, is an object of a special kind of knowledge: *noetic knowledge.*"

"I have been anxious to find out how God exists, as well as the extent to which we can speak of Him, or about Him, intelligibly only because I wanted to understand the basis and object of prayer: to whom do we pray? Do people pray to God himself, as a being with whom we can communicate? This question has been troubling me every time I pray in church and at home."

"Although it is difficult to assert that people pray to God himself, it is possible to say that they pray to Him because the light that shines through His presence in the universe flows from Him. This light is sacred because it is His light. Therefore, the church is a holy place, but every part of the universe is equally holy! This is why we should respect plants, animals, and matter!"

"It seems to me, Jirji, that you have introduced, in the view, you have just expounded, a new concept of divine creation—creation by emanation. God did not create the universe in one act or by uttering a word or by making a certain gesture. On the contrary, his original word is an on-going process of creation or emanation from his essential being."

"Yes, what you have just said follows as a logical inference from the analysis of the concept of emanation or immanence. The point I would like to underscore is that, from my perspective, it is reasonable to claim that God transcends the universe while being immanent in it at the same time. He transcends it by virtue of the transcendence of His essence, which surpasses the power of human cognition, and He is immanent in it through his light, or presence, that permeates the totality of the universe. This conception of God provides a strong ontological basis for the claim that the universe is co-eternal with God."

"I understand your account of the way that God is immanent in the universe and the sense in which He and the universe are co-eternal. Now can we return to our original question: how do we know about God? Can we say that the universe has a cause if we do not know the kind of cause He represents? Here, I mean the cause in itself. For example, we cannot say it is inferior in magnitude to the universe. It must be something greater than the universe. Can you conceive what it would be like for something to be greater than the universe? For example, the sun is greater than the moon or that the human giant is greater than the dwarf. Now think of the universe as an object, even though it is difficult to conceive. What kind of being can the cause of this universe be?"

"An answer to this question must originate from and be founded, as we saw earlier, in reflection on the natural and human worlds. These two worlds must necessarily reflect something about the nature of the cause. For example, light reflects, to some extent, the nature of the sun, although the sun is greater than the light that emanates from it. But, as the cause of the universe, God is greater than the universe not only in magnitude, in the sense that He possesses the power to create the universe, but also greater in every conceivable manner. Consequently, Nadim, when I say that we do not experience God directly in Himself, in the fullness of His essence, sensuously or intellectually, or that He does not exist entirely for us as an object, we can nevertheless learn about Him indirectly by contemplating the human and natural worlds, primarily because He is immanent in them. I should rush to add that the preceding line of reasoning is based on the assumption that the effect derives its nature from the cause which produces it. Can a human being, under normal conditions, procreate a cat or an apple tree? Can fire produce ice? Again, is the human being not evident in their actions or the artist in their work?"

"What your argument has shown is that we can gain some knowledge about God but not about God in Himself as you have just admitted. Is it possible to have *an encounter* with Him? What does it mean to say that we can have an encounter with a being when we do not stand before Him in the totality of His being?" Jirji's eyes flashed a cordial smile toward his cousin, and he said:

"This is the greatest challenge of any inquirer into the nature of God. And yet, although our knowledge of Him is incomplete, the knowledge we do have is genuine; it is *of Him*. Do I know a friend, a philosopher, a leader, even myself completely? Can I? Can we deny that our knowledge of this or that artist, or philosopher, or brother, or wife, or lover is trivial when we happen to have a genuine experience with any one of them? Does the theologian who taught me so much about St. Augustine know him or his teaching in the fullness of its essence? On the other hand, don't we conduct much of our thinking and acting based on such knowledge? I tend to think that we should be modest and honest with ourselves in any claim we make about ourselves, others, human life, and the world in general. These and similar reflections, Nadim, prompt me to say that standing before the light of the divine, and indeed in it, can provide an authentic encounter with it. If this type of experience can be an encounter, then prayer is a meaningful and justifiable encounter. However, I should emphasize here that the purpose of this event is not to ask God for a favor, to thank Him for something that happened in my life, or to make a confession of some kind. During this event, we can recognize the glory, magnificence, and abundance of the goodness of God. It should also be an occasion to understand our relationship with Him, to grow in our appreciation of this abundance, and, finally, to grow in our understanding of the world and ourselves. It is, in short, to become better human beings.

"Have you reflected on the wisdom that underlies the design of this amazing cosmos? Have you confronted the mystery that permeates the fabric of this design? Have you contemplated the dynamics of human nature and its creation in art, philosophy, science, culture, and social organization? Have you pondered the mystery of love, human presence, and the remarkable powers of the human mind? Have you wondered about how the human mind knows, creates ideas, relations, and images? More importantly, have you wondered about the mystery of consciousness and self-consciousness or why the human mind seeks God? Frankly, the mere reflection on these and related questions prompts me to stand in fear, respect, love, admiration, and appreciation of the cause that created, and continues to create, this wondrous machine known as the cosmos."

"I confess to you, Jirji, that I have not reflected on these questions, and I doubt that many, and perhaps the majority of people who pray to God, now and in the past, have reflected on them either. But suppose the kind of knowledge we have of God justifies the event of prayer, what kind of experience should it be? Is it necessary?

"No, but it is desirable."

"Why?"

"Because it is not an obligation. No legitimate authority, not even God, requests, demands, or obliges us to glorify him."

"But, then, how do you justify a prayer of glorification?"

"The same way we justify the praise or glorification of our superiors—teachers, parents, heroes, scientists, artists, or social reformers."

"I see. But prayer is a dialogical encounter, and if it is, what kind of dialogue takes place between the individual and God? But if it is not, what happens then? For example, the Christian says the Lord's Prayer in church or at home— what happens in this kind of event? With whom does the person who says it has a dialogue? Does God know whether it originates from their mind and heart? How would He accept or reject it?"

"The different types of prayer people say in church or at home are not really prayers. This is not only because God is not a mega human being with whom we can have a dialogue, but especially because He did not request it, as I emphasized more than once earlier."

"But, then, what does it mean to pray to a god if we do not know him and with whom we cannot have a direct encounter?"

"Let me *propose to* you that prayer is not merely a statement, or some kind of request, but rather an act of love—a love of God—and that this act should form the basis of human love of oneself and of the other person. I emphasize the first type of love because it is the source of all types of human love."

"What do you mean by 'love' in this context?"

"Love is an act in which we promote the spiritual and material wellbeing of oneself and other people. Although the medium of the loving act is emotion or feeling because it originates from the heart and the intuitive understanding of the situation we find ourselves in, the loving act is not an emotional act; it is essentially a rational act because it aims at the growth and development of the person we love."

"But if God is not a mega human being, how can we love Him?"

"We love Him by living according to the fundamental moral values that originate from the essence of human nature. This essence is one of the most, if not the *most luminous ray of God's presence* in the universe. How can we love another human being if the loving act is not founded in the fundamental precepts of love? And, how can these precepts be truly moral if they do not reflect the brilliance of this ray? The point I should underscore here is that the more we grow in loving other human beings, the more we love them, the more we promote the kind of love God intended in the essential needs of human nature the way they are revealed in the achievements of human beings individually, as well as in the course of history. We should always remember that love constructs, hate destroys. Love is the essence of good, hate is the essence of human evil."

"I follow your line reasoning even though you expounded your view succinctly," Nadim intervened. "Now, in what sense is the event of prayer an act of love? But, first, how does one glorify or express one's appreciation for the abundance of His creative activity, for the abundance of His giving? Before whom do we stand in this kind of event?"

"We stand before the universe as the unity of the natural and human orders, not as an idea and not as an object, although this is not easy to do, but as a dynamic, living reality, *as an emanation of the eternal presence of God.*"

"This time, your succinct answer eludes my understanding. Can you explain it?"

"First, I stand before God in so far as we stand in the light of His presence, which shines in and through the universe. During this stance, I acknowledge the enormity, the mystery, the magnificence, the sublimity, therefore, the sacredness of this presence. I also acknowledge the ultimacy of the wisdom that underlies it, and as the source of my being and life. Moreover, I acknowledge that my existence as a human being is a precious gift, a gift I should cherish, nourish, appreciate, and respect. This multivalent acknowledgment is, I think, the fountain of the greatest joy in my life. What does the genuine artist, scientist, mystic, philosopher, and living human being in general desire, and dare I say crave, but to feel and stand in this luminous presence? Why do these people frown upon the glory and pleasures of the world and devote themselves to the creative act? And what is this act but an act of love? Now, what is the source and substance of this love?"

"Do you imply that true prayer is a kind of celebration?"

"Yes, but my dear Nadim, every active, constructive, productive moment in our lives should be an occasion for celebration. Don't we enjoy the gifts we receive from friends and family members on festive events? Don't we celebrate the gift of life at birthday celebrations? Don't these gifts arouse in us emotions of love and appreciation for the person who gives them? Now, what are the gifts we receive on such occasions compared to the gift of life? Don't you think that the gift of life should be viewed as the greatest gift and that expressing our appreciation for it should be the greatest celebration?

"I should at this point of our conversation point out that, although this kind of prayer is voluntary and no one will reward or punish us if we say it, nonetheless, it remains an obligation—"

"An obligation?" Nadim blurted impulsively.

"Yes, an obligation of recognition. It originates from the bosom of the human condition the way all other types of obligations originate."

"What do you mean when you speak of obligation of recognition?"

"First, let me remind you that all the moral obligations we recognize and respect during daily life originate from the particular situations we find ourselves in. The obligations that are imposed by an external authority, such as society, reason, God, and the church, are abstract and therefore empty, for example, 'Be honest!', 'Love your fellow human being,' or 'Do not steal.' But the real question is, how do we identify particular situations of obligation? When should we feel this obligation? Under what conditions should I feel it? Who decides that I should act in a specific way in a particular moral situation? You see, moral obligations originate from the practical situations that arise during practical life, and no one can determine their nature and justifiability except the person who is intimately involved in the situation. Others may judge that I am under the obligation to act in a specific manner, but let me say that obligations are individual, they are not transferrable; they always remain personal and subjective."

"Next, moral obligation is neither emotional, nor idiosyncratic, or arbitrary. It arises from a complex web of social, cultural, legal, intellectual, religious, and psychological factors such as rules, norms, practices, customs, and personal experiences. The moral obligation arises from the worldview of the moral agent. At the center of this view is a certain moral consciousness. The feeling of obligation stems from an active response of this consciousness to the moral demand inherent to the situation. This mode of origination is what bestows upon the action its moral character. Mere conformity of an action to a particular command or rule does not necessarily make it moral. It may be a good action, one that promotes some good in the life of someone, but it will be an action without a moral soul.

"Accordingly, when I say that the obligation to pray is an obligation of recognition, I mean that it arises from the realization that God is the source of everything that exists: the universe, my life, as well as the aesthetic, moral, religious, intellectual, and social values that underlie the rise and development of human civilization, and also from the recognition that these values originate from His divine presence. Do I need to comprehend the essence of the sun to know that the light that emanates from it illuminates my life? A prayer that grows out of this recognition is a prayer that grows out of a religious heart, a heart that acts religiously not because a specific authority commanded it but because the individual who feels the obligation knows and believes in the absolute validity of the values that originate from the essence of our humanity.

"Don't we value a gift we receive when we know that the person who offered it does not have an ulterior or selfish motive, but instead acts out of respect and love? Don't we rejoice when we receive such a gift? And don't we celebrate this event? Why shouldn't we celebrate, at least once in a while, receiving the gift of life every morning when the sun spreads its light over our city? Don't you think, Nadim, that this type of recognition justifies the obligation to glorify God?"

Nadim's eyes were literally glued to Jirji's when he raised his last rhetorical question. Nick, who was watching his cousins submerged in this lengthy conversation, much of which he did not care to understand, intervened: "How about continuing this conversation at Spiro's? Abraham's request to spend the evening with him and Hanania have overridden my plan to go out this evening. I hope you can come to lunch with us, Jirji. I do not plan to attend the burial, but you can leave us at your convenience."

"That is absolutely fine with me!" Jirji said. His response was seconded by Nadim.

"Do I have a choice?" Johannes asked with a friendly smile

"I am afraid you do not!" Jirji responded with an equally jovial grin.

Before leaving the courtyard, Nick remarked in a rather low voice that the young ladies of the Mitya family were spying on them from the veranda upstairs. "Apparently, your conversation with Nadim sparked their curiosity, Jirji."

"But, we are family!" Jirji remarked.

"Some people are curious." Nick retorted.

"Or maybe they want us to leave so that they can clean the courtyard and the wailing room."

"A person without curiosity really suffers from a dull intellect!" Jirji said, and changing the subject, he asked:

"How about taking one last look at Uncle Mikhail?"

"I have no desire to look at that loathsome face again. Looking at it will kill my appetite!"

"Be kind!" Jirji said.

"Why don't you all take a look at it? I shall wait for you in the hallway."

Together, Nadim, Jirji, and Johannes went to the funeral chamber, stood next to the coffin, and said a silent prayer.

THREE

Mikhail Mitya's Secret

ALTHOUGH THE GENERAL ATMOSPHERE at the Mitya residence was gloomy that morning, it was cheerful at Spiro's restaurant. A national attraction for seafood, this restaurant overlooked the Mediterranean Sea and was separated from the ocean by a cornice and a narrow road. The golden rays of the sun, which descended upon the sea glittering like a sapphire in the vibrant beams of light, infused the afternoon air with an aura of gaiety. The landscape that stretched before the gazes of the cousins and their guest was exuberant and simply beautiful. Unlike Nick, Nadim, and Jirji, who sat down in their chairs as soon as they arrived, mainly because they were familiar with the restaurant and the seashore, Johannes remained standing for a few moments contemplating the beauty of the sea. It was clear to Jirji that he was deeply impressed by the mystical dialogue between the sky, the sun, the sea, and the vibrant beams of light. "Latakia is a beautiful city!" Johannes said when he sat, and with his eyes still absorbed in the dance, he added, "The Latakia shoreline is splendid! No wonder the ancient gods chose to live on the high mountains that overlooked the Mediterranean!" Those words ambushed Jirji's ears with surprising force, causing his eyes to abruptly abandon the menu he was reading and leap onto the figure of his guest. Their eyes met; they were locked in a silent, and undefinable, dialogue. They spoke eloquently, lucidly. I suspect that their conversation proceeded like this: "Have you seen what I have seen?"

"Yes, I have!"

"Have you felt what I felt?"

"I have."

What other type of dialogue, if any, was possible, could have transpired between those pairs of eyes and those two hearts? Johannes, who sat across the table from him, ceased to be a stranger, and he ceased to be a cousin, regardless of whether he was, in fact, his cousin. He sat before him as a human being, as a *flare of humanity*. What does it mean for a person to be a cousin, a brother, a sister, or even a parent if that person is not a flare of humanity? But Jirji did not speak with the stranger merely with his mind but also with his heart, for a gush of warmth surged into his heart at that moment. He felt alive, and he felt the thrill created in his heart by that gush of heat, and he felt a strong desire to luxuriate in it.

When that kind of gush whirls in your heart, your eyes see with a new vision, and your mind thinks with the fire surging from that moment. For some strange reason, the fountain of giving opens up in your heart. Love flows from it freely, abundantly. The guest who contemplated the mystery of the divine dance on the shimmering blue sea a moment ago must have been in his upper twenties. His hair was blond, and his eyes were blue. He was a handsome young man. It seemed to Jirji that he was steeped in the mysteries of the human mind. Refinement and thoughtfulness were the distinctive features of his complexion. There was nothing ordinary and nothing malicious about him. He was soft-spoken, but he spoke with an air of confidence and determination.

Jirji never imagined, not even in his wildest dreams, that he would encounter a human being who could see and delight in the dance of the infinite on the shimmering ripples of the Mediterranean, and yet, that very human being was standing before him watching that glorious dance. The mere recognition of this fact gave birth to an unshakeable bond with that human being. "There is something mysterious, something seductive about this side of the Mediterranean," Johannes remarked when he sat down next to Nadim.

"Yes," Jirji returned with a heaving chest. Apparently, the gush of warmth that was whirling in his heart must have lingered there. He did not wish it to leave that sanctuary, but the situation he was in obviated this possibility.

"And, there is something mysterious about Johannes as well!" Nick interrupted his cousin. Surprised, Jirji and Johannes thrust a questioning look at Nick, but he neither saw nor heard his cousin's response. In contrast, Nadim, who must have felt that a scandalous confrontation between Nick and Johannes was about to flare up, stared at Jirji with pleading eyes, as if to beg him to subvert this possibility. "No one has ever mentioned or talked about a German branch of the family. I would like to know about them." Nick continued.

"I shall be happy to answer any question you might have, Uncle Nick."

"Uncle!" Nick murmured in a hardly audible whisper.

"But first tell me –if you arrived in Latakia a month ago, why didn't you try to contact anyone of us during this time? What is particularly baffling to me is that you have gone to his house and visited Uncle Mikhail—correct?"

"Yes."

"And you seem to know a great deal about us. Only God knows how much. And yet, you have not made the slightest effort to meet any of your uncles and cousins. Any ordinary person would be confused, and in fact, offended by your behavior, even if the Mitya family in Germany is a genuine descendant of Patriarch Abraham, as you claim. Your behavior is unrealistic; it goes against the grain, against any family norm, against commonsense."

This aggressive interrogation produced three different reactions in the three cousins. Nadim was sympathetic to Nick and, in fact, he agreed with him, but he thought that Nick was a bit hard on Johannes, almost belligerent. Moreover, he felt that his cousin's questions were to the point and that the interrogation was forceful. Jirji, on the other hand, thought that there was no need for Nick to be combative not only because Johannes was being treated as a guest but also because answers to all of Nick's questions could be elicited rationally and courteously. However, the conversation was interrupted by the sudden appearance of the waiter.

"Let me tell you about the specials first," the waiter said.

"That is a good idea," Jirji responded.

"Our best catches this morning were sultan fish in large and baby sizes. We were also able to catch some shrimp. They will be excellent with a Latakia garlic whip or lemon sauce, fried potato, and Armenian salad."

"What do you think, Johannes?"

"I am really anxious to try the sultan fish in both sizes, if possible. I have heard so much about the Swaydieh sultan, but never about the Latakia sultan. What is the difference between them?"

"As far as I know, there is no difference between them. The Latakia and Swaydieh seas are one and the same. They are separated by a legal line, but this line does not apply to the fish," Jirji said with a smile!

"I too would like the special. No fish in this area surpasses the taste and tenderness of the sultan. They did not name it 'The Sultan' by accident."

"Would you like a drink?" The waiter asked.

"Araq for me," Nick said.

"Would you like a drink, Johannes?" Jirji asked.

"Yes, please, a glass of beer."

"And a glass of beer for me," Jirji said to the waiter. Nadim also requested a glass of araq.

The departure of the waiter left a lull around the table. While Nick was expecting some kind of answer to his question, Jirji, who felt without a shred of doubt that Johannes was honest and that he must have a justifiable reason for delaying his visit to his cousins in Latakia, decided to give him a chance to speak, "You are right, Nick," Johannes said, "My tardiness in meeting my family here in Latakia is inexcusable, and has certainly exposed me to the charge of callousness, if not impertinence. I truly wish I could have avoided this charge—"

"Were you in an accident, difficulty, or an unhappy situation?" Jirji asked with a palpable feeling of concern.

"No, the first thing I did when I found an apartment was to get settled. This was not an arduous task, mainly because my possessions and needs were very modest. I lead a very simple life."

"But, then," Nick, who was indifferent to his cousin's feeling of concern and impatient with his guest, retorted, "What happened? Why—?"

"Please, Nick," Jirji interrupted, "give Johannes a chance to speak!"

"Well," Johannes said with a painfully contemplative expression on his face, "The Schumans, who knew Uncle Mikhail very well, told me that my grand Uncle was very sick and that he would certainly die in a few weeks. My immediate reaction was to see him. Salim, who noticed how I felt, offered to bring me to his house in the evening. I declined his offer and told him that I would take the bus, but he urged me to wait a little longer only because he knew where my Uncle lived and, more importantly, because he wanted to speak with me about some private and confidential matters. It was difficult to refuse his proposal."

"But if he brought you to Uncle Mikhail's house, why did you refrain from visiting Abraham and Hanania. They lived upstairs." Nick, who was anxious to prosecute his guest there and then said, interrupting Johannes.

"Your question" Uncle Nick "is logical," Johannes said in a cordial and very respectful manner. "The door was open when I arrived at the house.

Aunt Rachel was upstairs. She lived with her sons, not with her husband, as I soon discovered. Uncle Mikhail was stunned to see me when I knocked at the open door of his room. He regarded me with an expression of displeasure, for he thought that I was a thief or some kind of intruder. But I soon allayed his fears, assuring him that I was a Mitya and that I was his grandnephew—"

"My grandnephew?" He interrupted me with a somewhat disbelieving voice and was suddenly assaulted by an intense coughing fit during which he ejected some blood into a spittoon that was placed next to his bed. I watched him cough and spit blood in the jar with an aching heart. He did not have any teeth. His head was bald, and his white beard was unshaven. He needed urgent attention, I thought. But this train of thought was checked by another, sharper episode of coughing. When he finished driveling his bloody saliva into the jar, he said with tears in his eyes, "I am sorry, son! You are a young man. You should not witness a dying man in my condition.'"

"Please, your condition is more common than you think. I am not a stranger to it. Do not rush. Take your time."

"Are you—?" He could not complete his sentence because yet another fit of coughing arrived. I tried to pacify him. "Can I do anything to help?" I asked.

"No, son,'" he had said in a hoarse voice. "'I shall be dying in two or three weeks at most. This is what the doctor told me.'" A shiver ran through my body.

"Do not rush!" I said. "Take your time. I am not in a hurry, Uncle."

"'Uncle!'" Mikhail exclaimed. "You speak with a Swaydieh dialect. Not many members of the family here, especially the young generation, speak it. You cannot be from Swaydieh because all my brothers left that village a long time ago. George, Deeb, and Chick went to America. Habib died in his early forties, and your grandfather went to Europe, but no one knows where he settled."

"He went to Germany," I said.

"To Germany?"

"Yes, I know."

"How do you know all this?"

"My grandfather, Hanania, told me."

"Hanania?" Mikhail screamed, but his scream was aborted by another episode of coughing. When he regained his composure, he pinned me with a hard look and said, "You look like your grandfather!"

"Yes, everyone says so."

Uncle Mikhail stretched out his feeble, trembling arms and tried to embrace me. He could not, but I embraced him. We lingered in that embrace for a few moments. "Bring a chair and sit near me!" Tears were flowing from his eyes when I was placing the chair next to his bed. He could not wipe the tears because another fit of coughing visited him. It was clear to me that he was overwhelmed by my sudden appearance at that moment in his life. A dead past, pleasant and unpleasant, must have crept into his consciousness. He was contemplative for a few seconds.

"Hanania went to Germany, then."

"Then, you should remember him quite well."

"Yes, I do. You are the youngest, and he was the oldest among Patriarch Abraham's six sons." My uncle nodded and then added, "you are the most intelligent, most courageous, and kindest of all the brothers. You were his favorite brother, and he loved you more than anyone in the whole family. He also told me, among other things, good ones I should say, that you were an honorable man and did all you could to protect and help any member of the family. He relayed to me the story of how you rushed to his defense against two men who tried to denigrate him because you and he were the sons of a butcher. Even though you were younger than them, you beat them and scared them away. You darted into the belly of one of them like a rocket so fast, and so hard he cowered with a shriek, and then you punched him in the face, made his nose bleed, and told him with a threatening voice that if he ever came near your brother, you would crush him. When the other man saw what you did, he ran away as fast as his legs allowed.'"

"Is this how you remember this anecdote, Uncle?' Mikhail smiled and nodded. "Yes, your grandfather and I had many good times together, but we were separated by the cruel hand of fate. Life was very hard in those days. My father was unable to support us. The Great Depression destroyed the livelihood of many families. Not knowing where your grandfather went, or whether he was dead or alive, tore my heart to pieces. The only thing we could do was to secure our future in a different county. People would board any ship they found and travel without knowing where they were going. They were allowed to get on board a ship on the condition that they worked in the kitchen, the engine room, or the cleaning department. This is how they traveled. I boarded a cargo ship in Beirut and landed in New York six months later. Time was cheap, but human life was cheaper! Anyway, I worked in the kitchen. I was a good cook. My father was a butcher for the Ottoman army. He taught me how to cut meat and how to cook it."

Uncle Mikhail abruptly stopped, pressed his lips hard, and then frowned. Another fit of coughing was on its way. He tried to swallow his saliva, but he could not, then he tried to clear his throat. He could not! He simply stared at me with wide eyes, eyes brimming with tears. To my great surprise, for I had never spent time with a man dying from cancer in the lungs, my uncle exploded into a violent fit of coughing. He reached for the spittoon, but he could not grasp it. I rushed to it and held it close to his mouth. Clots of blood poured into it with every cough. He filled it within a few seconds. I looked around for a sink but did not know which way to go, for I was still ignorant of the design of the house. He was able to point to the kitchen, across the courtyard where Nick, Nadim, and Jirji had their conversation during the funeral a week later. I emptied the blood in the sink and washed it with soap. Uncle Mikhail was struggling with the pillows against which he reclined. They were jumbled when he was coughing.

"Let me adjust them for you, Uncle!"

"Please, upright."

"Certainly!"

"You see, I cannot breathe, and I cannot sleep on my sides because if I do, I choke."

"I understand, Uncle. Here you are!" I said after I was done. An involuntary sigh flew stealthily from his mouth when he sat on his bed. He embraced me with a loving look.

"The cancer has spread through my lungs. It is eating me up slowly. This is my fate. I do not deserve to die this kind of death and in this kind of condition."

I did not know how to react to this painful admission, and yet I could not resist placing my hand on my uncle's shoulder. I caressed it gently. He felt my fingers, and he must have felt the compassion that was transmitted from my heart to his heart. Although what I did was spontaneous, and perhaps what he needed, a light but clean cough escaped from his throat when he leaned against his pillows. "You are not my grandnephew," he said, "you must be an angel from heaven," and then, focusing his eyes on the open window of the vault, he continued, "or maybe from your grandfather in heaven." He threw an affectionate look at me and added, "he must be

35

in heaven. This is where good people go after they die. They cannot go anywhere else."

"How long have you been ill?" I asked, interrupting his rumination—"

But Johannes was unable to continue his narrative because a two-level cart accompanied by two waiters stopped next to their table. Within a few seconds, they placed the plates and the drinks on the table. "Bon appetite," one of the waiters said. He looked at Jirji and whispered, "If you need anything, just wave your hand!"

"Thank you, Farooq!" Jirji cast a glance at the table and added, "Although it is a sad day for me because we lost a member of the Mitya family, it is also a blessed day because we gained a new member. Let us have a toast in honor of our new cousin, Johannes!" Johannes lifted his glass and said, "I am deeply grateful to meet my new cousins and to share this sad day with you! May we have a toast in memory of our Uncle, Mikhail. I do appreciate your good sentiments, Jirji!"

Three beer and araq glasses connected with a soft click. The fourth glass remained on the table. Oblivious to what was happening around him, Nick was frantically eating his food. Frankly, he was indifferent to his cousins. It was evident that he was displeased with Jirji's and Nadim's welcoming attitude toward their newly discovered cousin.

"The Latakia sultan is truly delectable! My grandfather was not amiss when he said that it was the best fish in this region of the Mediterranean," Johannes remarked.

"I am glad you are enjoying it!" Nadim said, but he and Jirji were directing frequent glances at Nick. His grouchiness was conspicuous to them, as well as Johannes. It was an embarrassing situation, Jirji thought. He waved to the waiter. "Can we have another round of drinks, Farooq?"

"Of course!" He replied.

"It is a good occasion," Jirji observed after the waiter left.

"If you have seen Uncle Mikhail every evening during the past two weeks," Nick continued his interrogation, "and if you knew that he was going to die, yes, you seem to know so much about us, why did you avoid us and especially Aunt Rachel and her sons? I would just like to know why? A man who loves his granduncle so much but shies away from his nephews, sons, and aunt is weird, indeed bewildering, to say the least. Your behavior boggles my mind."

"But, Nick—"

"Why don't you let Johannes answer my question, Jirji? Please, I love you very much, and you know it. This time I beg you to let him answer my question." Jirji bit his lower lip and complied with Nick's request. It seemed to him that Nick was not listening carefully to Johannes's account of the first part of his visit to his uncle and especially what happened during that visit. Nadim was embarrassed; he felt that Nick should be controlled and that the only person who could accomplish this was Jirji. He moved his right foot forward and landed a forceful step on Jirji's foot, who understood the meaning of his cousin's action and responded to it with a soft nod.

"Let me repeat it, Uncle Nick," Johannes said, "that your questions are logical. You have the right to doubt the authenticity of my lineage, as well as my grandfather's. Why should you believe that I am your cousin without credible evidence?"

"Yes, evidence!" Nick returned.

"But please do not treat me as a defendant in a court of law. I am not a lawyer, although I know a little about the legal system in Germany." He said with a touch of humor in his voice.

"I too am not a lawyer, and I do not like lawyers."

"Justice would go back to the jungle without them," Johannes remarked.

"Then we must be in the jungle. The only difference between the two jungles is one of degree and style. The first follows the laws of nature, while the second follows the laws of the powerful."

"The powerful?" Johannes exclaimed.

"Yes, because they govern the different societies of the world. It will be a long, long time before humanity is ready for the laws of reason! What is sad is that the laws of the powerful are the laws of nature in disguise."

"That is a debatable question."

"I simply express my opinion. Frankly, I cannot defend it."

"I appreciate your honesty very much, Uncle Nick!"

"Now let me reveal to you and to my cousins," Johannes said, "that I was visiting Uncle Mikhail
every evening during the past few weeks—"

"Every evening, during the past two weeks?" Nick ejaculated with an evident tone of irritation.

"Yes, every evening—"

"And without contacting any of us, not even Uncle Mikhail's sons or mother?" Nick almost shouted.

"Please calm down a little, Uncle Nick. I shall answer all your questions, and I shall explain everything I said in case it seems vague or their dubious to you."

"You and your way of doing things, Johannes, are strange."

"Am I strange, or is Uncle Mikhail's situation strange?"

"Why don't you give the man a chance to speak, Nick?" Jirji intervened. "I shall!"

"At the end of my first visit to him, Uncle Mikhail asked me to visit him the next evening. I gladly complied with his request. He then asked me to keep our visits confidential."

"Confidential? Why?" I wondered in the silence of my mind. I frowned and was about to decline his request. Although he was very sick, in fact, dying, his eyes were very sharp. He noticed my frown, and he understood its cause. 'I feel at home with you. I have not had this feeling in many, many years, son. Don't deprive the luxury of this feeling from a dying man. My mind and heart have been captive to loneliness for a long time. Loneliness is hell on earth, and dying in its desert is the worst kind of hell! I feel a strong urge to speak, to open up to a person who empathizes, who understands, who forgives. Ah, my son, he continued with a mournful sigh, I see my brother in you: I see his compassionate heart, his kindness, in you. I wish to spend the evening hours with you rather than with the darkness of this vault. Do you know that when I cough in this darkness, I feel like I am coughing in my grave? More than once, I felt as if I were already dead. Please, son, brighten this vault with your presence!'"

"There is no need to relay the remainder of this speech, but I think that what I communicated to you should give you an idea of the reason that prompted me to honor his request. You might think that I was wrong in granting him his request. I doubt that any decent human being would deny it. However, if you think that I was mistaken in what I did, you can reprimand me. I shall gladly accept your rebuke, even my dismissal from your company, but I shall not feel remorseful over the decision I made—"

"Why didn't you see him during the day?" Nick resumed his interrogation

"Because no family member, neighbor, or friend knocked at his door during the evening. The only member of the family he remembered with a feeling of appreciation was Jameela, Hanania's wife. She cooked soft dishes he could chew, since he had no teeth, and she always made sure that he had at least two meals a day."

"And his children?" Nadim asked with a quivering voice.

"Yes, he mentioned them. Abraham saw him in the morning once or twice a week. He never spent more than two or three minutes with him, but Hanania called upon him mostly twice a day, mainly to ascertain if he had enough pain killers. 'They came and left, but in truth, they never came, and they never left.' He once mumbled, but I heard what he said."

"And the grandchildren?" Nadim pressed on.

"They ignored his existence. Uncle Mikhail thought that Abraham discouraged them from seeing him. 'He was embarrassed by his father—' Uncle Mikhail said in a very sorrowful voice.

"But what about his wife?" Nadim interjected.

"She shunned him like the plague. These were Uncle Mikhail's words."

"Like the plague?" Nadim ejaculated vehemently. "Can it be? How can it be?"

Johannes fired a hard, inquisitive look at Nadim. The message of his gaze was this: "Why? Why are you so surprised?"

"Because she acts like she is the most loving mother in the world, and because her children presented her to the family as a saintly woman. They are devoted to her. They worship the ground on which she walks. No one can contradict what she says or criticize what she does. She is always right. No one of the in-laws or the children dares offend her. As far as I know, no member of the extended family has complained about or criticized her regarding anything she said or did. Her image among both the younger and older generation is that of a compassionate, nurturing, and protective mother."

But Jirji, who has so far been silent, interjected, "How can a saint act this way? How can the children of a saint act this way? Aren't we supposed to love our enemies and forgive those who have wronged us?"

"I am glad you have reminded us of what Jesus Christ has said, but it does not apply to your uncle because he is not a human being. Show me a human being, a real one, I mean, who abandons his wife and two toddlers, who wastes his life in the most sinful way, who leads this way of life knowingly, voluntarily, and I show you a brute! Your Uncle, Jirji, renounced his humanity a long time ago. Not every person who walks on two feet and speaks a human language is necessarily a human being."

"Don't you think that you are unnecessarily harsh on your uncle? Can a human being renounce their humanity? Is a person not given to the world as a human being the same way they are given ears and eyes? Can the stone choose to be a rose? It is more appropriate for you to inquire about the real reasons for his ostracism by his family."

"What you have just said on behalf of Uncle Mikhail, Johannes," Nadim said, flustered, "is confusing. How can a woman be heartless and heartful at the same time? But what baffles my mind is how no member of the family, not even Abraham or Hanania, have ever noticed, pointed out, or mentioned this blatant contradiction in Aunt Rachel's character."

This last exchange between Johannes and Nadim elicited a sarcastic, and one might add malicious, chuckle from Nick. The three cousins looked at him, curiosity plain in their eyes. Sarcastic gestures are not typically expressed in a vacuum but as a response to a recalcitrant question, enigma, paradox, or something absurd or ridiculous. Could Nick have allowed this chuckle to escape without an adequate reason? The cousins wanted to hear such reasons, for they looked at him with inquisitive eyes, and in fact Nick was willing to deliver an explanation. "I do not see any enigma or paradox in Aunt Rachel's character," he said. "Uncle Mikhail was the most despicable human being and the most contemptible husband in the city of Latakia. As far as I know, no angel, and indeed no devil, would like to come close to him. Thank god, he is dead. The family is now free from this moral cancer. How can you blame a wife if she shuns such a husband?"

"I am quite aware that the family treated him as a bad person, that he had been ostracized not only by them but also by friends and neighbors. But to confess, I do not know why his wife and children treated him as *persona non grata*—like an outcast. I now feel that other people shunned him more based on hearsay, on family gossip, on some kind of bias than based on authentic facts. You seem to know much more about our departed Uncle, Nick, than any of us—can you please shed some light on the reasons that prompted his wife and children to ostracize him?"

"Gladly!" Nick replied. "As I mentioned this morning, Uncle Mikhail was a philanderer, a drunkard, and an adulterer. He was well known in the community for his sexual conquests. Even some members of the Mitya women were his victims. He slept with women without knowing who they were! You should know this, Nadim. My neighbor, Elias Bandar, told me with tears in his eyes that Uncle Nick was the Casanova of Latakia. If you kick him out the door, he returns through the window and seduces the woman of the house. He would sleep only with married women. Tell me, Nadim, what wife would sleep in the same bed with such a husband?

"Your uncle was the worst drinker in town. He used to begin drinking as soon as he returned from the silk factory. The liquor stores can tell you stories about him. One of them, Andrews, who was a friend of cousin Abraham, told me that he would drink half a pint of straight araq in one gulp. He would stop, cough a little, have a morsel of country cheese, and then drink the other half also in one gulp. He always bought another pint and hid it in the inner pocket of his pantaloon. He used to arrive at his house wasted. More than once, his son Abraham asked Andrews not to sell his father any kind of liquor; he even promised to pay him for the araq his father usually bought from him. 'If he does not buy it from me,' Andrews said to him more than once, 'he will buy it from another liquor store. At least I give him some bread and cheese and a piece of onion after he takes his first gulp.'" Uncle Mikhail began to drink heavily after his second son was born. At that time, his wife used to tell him to drink and enjoy his liquor but not to get drunk. Every time she asked him to drink moderately, he showered her with abusive words and left the house. Sometimes he returned in the middle of the night, and sometimes he slept somewhere else. Tell me, what decent wife would sleep in the same bed with a drunkard like this one?

"But this is not all. Shortly after the birth of his second son, Uncle Mikhail immigrated to America in search of a good job, the way his brothers did. He stayed in New York for three years. He never sent any money to his wife and children, not even a letter. When he returned to Latakia, he was penniless. I discovered from a Latakia immigrant who knew the Mitya brothers in New York that he was an idler most of the time. No factory would employ him for more than a few weeks because he was drunk most of the time. This immigrant said that his brothers gave him a hefty allowance and practically forced him to return to his wife and children. But he squandered the money on gambling and drinking and returned to his family without any money in his pocket!

"Has anyone in the family wondered, or cared to question, how this saint, Aunt Rachel, managed to survive and take care of her two sons? Frankly, only a few people know the history of her life. I am one of them. This woman worked as a maid. She saved every penny she earned to buy food and clothes for the children and herself. She was so ashamed of her situation that she practically avoided every social event, even church events. Her sons were the jewels of her life. What did your bankrupt Uncle do to fulfill his obligations as a father and husband? Nothing. His weekly salary was so meager he could barely pay the rent for the house. Anyway, he spent most of it on his liquor and mistresses. Let me tell you, Nadim, that this uncle of yours was a good-for-nothing Mitya. His history was riddled with one scandal after another. There is no need to burden your ears, or those of Jirji and Johannes with any further details about this human embarrassment.

"I know that respect for older people, and especially the Mitya elders, is an obligation. I observe this obligation, but I cannot respect Uncle Mikhail. I prefer to be sinful and pay for my sinful behavior rather than show respect for him—"

Nadim stood up at this juncture of Nick's explanation of why there was no contradiction in saying that Aunt Rachel was a saint and her refusal to attend to him when he was dying. "I need to go home and attend the funeral." Nadim said, "Nick, why don't you, Johannes, and Jirji continue this conversation? I would like to hear a synopsis of what transpired between you regarding Uncle Mikhail. Will you be attending the burial, Jirji? Johannes?" Both of them replied in the negative almost simultaneously.

"Then I shall see you at Abraham's and Hanania's house this evening." The cousins looked at one another and then at Johannes. "I feel enlightened by your defense of Aunt Rachel against her husband," Jirji said when Nadim left, "but I think that your description of his character is exaggerated, if not one-sided."

"What do you mean, Jirji? Can you explain the purport of your response?"

"Let me ask you: Has Uncle Mikhail maligned or stolen anything from any store, family member, or stranger?"

"Not that I know of."

"Has he gossiped about or slighted the character of any person?" Nick reflected on this question for almost a minute and then said no. "Now," Jirji continued, "has he denied any person, relative or stranger, any request for help?"

"I don't know of any such case."

"On the contrary," Jirji continued, "wasn't your Uncle in the forefront whenever any family member was threatened by a stranger or whenever any family member needed help?"

"He was always here, and he was the most valiant defender of the Mitya family. But the critical question, the incriminating question, is the despicable way he treated his wife and children. All those good qualities you tried to highlight would dim in significance compared to the atrocities of his behavior toward his wife and children.

"Are you sure?"

"I am." Nick said and turning his attention toward Johannes added with a cynical tone in his voice, "You visited Uncle Mikhail in the evening for a few weeks. I wonder whether he disclosed to you some knowledge about his life or his family's life."

"Yes, Uncle Mikhail was very close to my grandfather. He was his favorite brother. I am a historian, and I am intensely interested in the history of Syria, the land of my forefathers. I must know as much as I can about my family here in Latakia. This knowledge would enrich my understanding of myself. During his reminiscences, Uncle Mikhail told me much about his life and about the different Mitya families in Latakia. Frankly, even though he was deteriorating, his memory was excellent."

"Did he say anything about his wife and children?"

"Much."

"How much?"

"I think, that the knowledge he relayed to me about them is radically different from the knowledge you and the other members of the family have."

"How much?"

"I think that what I know might displease you." Nick's complexion suddenly changed. It assumed a garb of tense seriousness."

"How do you know I will be displeased?"

"I overheard the conversation you had with Uncle Nadim over the coffin of Uncle Mikhail. I was standing behind you, waiting for my turn to take one more look at the man who loved my grandfather more than anyone else. I was not snooping. I just could not prevent my ears from hearing your remarks. No one in my place could. Ears cannot discriminate between snooping and attentive listening, or any other type of listening for that matter."

"Then, you know what I think about Uncle Mikhail's relationship with his wife and children."

"Yes, I do."

"Then, go straight to the subject without any introductions or formalities," Nick said rather testily.

"Aunt Rachel is not the saint you and other family members think, and she is to blame for Uncle Mikhail's neglect of her and the children, and especially for his excessive drinking and philandering, as you repeatedly emphasized."

"She? You must be out of your mind, Johannes."

"Maybe, but let me tell you, Uncle Mikhail's side of the story."

"I am all ears!" Nick said, pursed his lips, and assumed the posture of a duelist.

"Shortly after Rachel became pregnant with her second son, Uncle Mikhail suspected that the child growing in his wife's womb was not his. Doubt maligned the deepest recesses of his mind. He battled with it for several days but ultimately could not bear it any longer. So, he went to the family midwife, who attended to the birth of all the Mitya children, confidentially expressed his doubts to her, and described in detail the conditions under which the child was supposed to have been conceived. She told him that his wife was most likely in her eighth month of pregnancy. 'No one can say with any certainty when she will give birth to the child, but, knowing the family, I can tell you that it will be at most two months from now.' The midwife looked at Mikhail with compassion and said, 'Mikhail, if you have any questions or if your wife has any problems, do not hesitate to let me know.'"

"For some reason, instead of receding to the back of his mind, doubt leaped to its front. Uncle Mikhail became restless and could not have sexual intercourse with his wife anymore. 'I lost my sexual appetite!' He said, 'you see, doubt kills not only sexual appetite but also the appetite for any kind of pleasure and sometimes numbs the desire for life itself.' His cheerfulness, for which he was well known among his friends and relatives, degenerated into a mood of seriousness, of reflectiveness. Aunt Rachel noticed this change in her husband but remained quiet about it until the child was born. Mikhail was present at its birth. His sister-in-law, Zaina, objected to his presence. "Men are not allowed at these events," she told him irritably.

"I can and will attend this event. This is my wife, and this child is my child, not yours. Don't worry, I shall not bother anybody.' Although reluctantly, she acquiesced to his request, as did the midwife who listened to the short interchange without saying a word. She knew she could not prevent Uncle Mikhail from witnessing the birth of his child, and she knew why.

"It was a boy. To his shock, the child looked frail and had very dark hair and dark brown eyes. The mere sight of the boy sent shivers through Uncle Mikhail's body. A mild tremble followed the shivers. He cast a quick glance at his wife. She had been eyeing him with fear in her heart when Uncle Mikhail was looking at the baby. When he looked at her, she avoided his eyes, but he kept his gaze fixed on her until she had no choice but to face him. Their eyes were clasped in a silent but dreadful conversation, and it was an abominable moment for my Uncle. His chin quivered, he clenched his teeth so hard that he almost splintered them into jots. The midwife, who was standing next to Aunt Rachel, noticed the silent dialogue. She knew the genetic history of the Mitya family. She understood the meaning of the exchange, she understood Uncle Mikhail's situation perfectly well, and she was convinced in the depth of her heart and mind that his wife cheated on him. Alas, how many similar cases had she treated? But she was not in a position to make any assertion. She moved slowly, almost imperceptibly, closer to Uncle Mikhail, held his arm, and led away from that scene. 'Patience!' She murmured when they were leaving the room. 'Things happen. We cannot resurrect any event or dead person from the past. Do not rush into any decision or action. You cannot prove with absolute certainty that he is not your child. If I were you, I would wait until the child is a teenager. He should have some of your physical features and some of his mother's, at least some of the features of his aunts and uncles on your side of the family. Even these cannot be the basis of a final judgment. Your parents, grandparents, and their children had blue eyes and blonde hair. In the future, you should look for psychological features. Don't neglect this factor. I am an old woman, and I shall not live for a long time. I doubt that I can assist you anymore."

"A few years later, the midwife died but not Uncle Mikhail's doubt and not his living misery. On the contrary, it was a constant nuisance, and because, like a ghost, it intruded into his mind whenever he tried to perform any kind of daily activity. He decided to wait, as the midwife had advised until the child became a teenager, but his waiting was torture: the minutes became hours, the hours days, the days weeks, and the weeks months. 'It became clear to me,' Uncle Mikhail said with tears in his eyes, 'that he was not a Mitya, not only in his physical features but also in the way he thought, played, ate, acted in school, and interacted with other children. I do not know whether anyone else saw what I saw, or even cared to see what I saw. He simply was an odd presence in my family and particularly in my life. I pitied the boy!' He paused a second to clear his throat and continued, 'But what if other family members noticed and discovered, or even doubted, what I knew, would they declare it? What did his mother think and feel every time she looked at him, dressed, or fed him?' Then wiping his tears with his shirt sleeve, he added, 'I want you to examine Hanania's physical features and compare them to Abraham's and other children in the family. Judge for yourself."

"I shall, Uncle," I said. "But how did you survive all this time? How did your wife react to the new way you behaved toward her?" Uncle Mikhail expressed the most sardonic chuckle you have ever witnessed.

"Not only love but also hate, yes, hate, can sometimes drive people to survive. In some cases, it is destructive; in others, it is constructive. In my case, it was destructive! Love drives the lover to pursue noble causes, and hate drives them to pursue ignoble causes. However, I am reluctant to tell you or anyone else how I acted and what kind of life I lived after I was absolutely certain that my wife was an adulterer."

"Why?"

"Because the way of life I led would strike any sensible person as unbelievable."

"But regardless of how complex or recalcitrant the truth is, it will be believable, in the future, if not now," I said. "No rational person can deny the truth, and no honest person can hide it. Try me, Uncle!"

"Be patient and, more importantly, son, be sympathetic."

"I shall be."

"Those who are in a problematic, and especially in a painful situation, think, feel, and act differently from those who observe it or read about it."

"I fully agree with you."

"When the doubt that Hanania was not my son concretized itself in my mind as an established belief, the first question I had to struggle with was why my wife refused to confess her crime to me? Did she think I would not know? Who can hide such crimes? I was a caring, attentive, and hard-working husband. Why would a wife betray such a husband? Our marriage contract was not only a legal document, but it was also a moral document, and it was blessed by the priest in front of friends and family members. Such an agreement is binding. The source of a moral obligation is moral conscience. A person without a moral conscience is not, and cannot be a genuine human being. Such a being cannot be trusted. She can easily betray me, other people, and even God. How can any man be a good husband to such a person?

"Do you know that although Hanania was innocent and did not choose the way he was born, and although I was kind and loving to him, to this day, he existed as a sharp thorn in my side, as a constant reminder of his mother's sin. Every time I looked at him, I saw an image of his mother sleeping with a man and lusting for another.'

"Did you try to speak with your wife about the authenticity of Hanania's birth or why she betrayed you?" He chuckled.

"No. What is the use of speaking with her about this or any other subject? It was she, not I, who should have disclosed the truth to me. But, since she did not, I felt reluctant to broach the subject. Had I spoken with her, the situation would have been very harmful to Hanania, to her, and to the entire family. It would have been like opening a big can of poisonous bees. I felt like I was standing on a rock in the middle of the sea; suddenly, the rock began to sink into its depths, and I was sinking with it.' Mikhail paused for a moment, cleared his throat, and made sure that a coughing fit was not forthcoming. 'Oh, no, some force pulled me up to the surface and helped me swim to the shore. Was it the power of hate? I wonder! But I was a completely different person when I stood on that shore and looked upward at the blue sky. Could it be God? I wonder! In truth, this radical transformation was, for me, tragic, because my desire for life, which I prized immensely, my love for my children, whom I was unable to love the way I wished and who was a profound source of pride and hope during the first few years of my married life, yes, they and everything that was dear to me remained in the sea when that rock sank into its bowels. I was bereft of my inner self. I began to see the world around me through the dark glasses of loneliness, hate, and cynicism. Slowly, I began to drink and smoke heavily, and I began to seduce women, not because I enjoyed having sex with them or because they were beautiful or alluring, for most of them were not beautiful, but from a feeling of revenge—revenge against my wife, against women in general. You may be shocked to know that behind the mask of purity, virtue, and religiosity men and women wear in public, you can easily find a sexual, psychological, and intellectual wolf. I saw my wife in every woman I slept with!'

"'But, what is sad, really sad, is that I distanced myself spatially and psychologically from my wife and children. I could not function as a good father and husband anymore. How can you, when you know without a shred of doubt that the woman who sleeps in your bed and cares for your children is a fraud? Every time I looked at Hanania, I saw a generic father— I saw an alien farther hovering before my eyes. This sight used to make me cringe. The strong desire, which lay in the back of my mind, would rise all the way to my throat and clasp it with its sharp claws. This kind of desire is psychological cancer. Do you know that this cancer is a curse?' Mikhail was suddenly lost in deep contemplation."

"Did you try to talk about how you felt and the kind of transformation you were experiencing with a cousin or a friend?" He smiled.

"You are in Latakia, not in Germany. Our society still lives in a cave of ignorance. The moment anyone knows that your wife cheated on you, you are ruined. You lose your dignity, your manhood, your identity, you lose the right to respect that every human being deserves. You become the talk of the town. And here, let me warn you, son: choose your words carefully when you speak with your cousins, uncles, and aunts. The Mitya family thrives on gossip, especially dirt, and scandalous rumors."

"Have you thought of consulting a psychologist?"

"That is worse."

"Why?"

"Because in this society only schizophrenics go to psychologists. The moment you see one, people will treat you as a crazy person, as a psychotic! No sane person, one who values their life, can admit that they suffer from a psychological discomfort or problem. You are always supposed to appear healthy, sane, happy, perfect, and the master of your life, otherwise you become a laughing stock among your family and friends. People here do not have any respect for the weak, the sick, and the poor. This is why you should always appear strong.'

"Have you thought of seeing a priest?"

"Oh, no! Priests are the most corrupt people in our society. A devil thrives behind the black robe they wear. What makes you think that Hanania is not the son of a priest?"

"But," Johannes said with a sad tone in his voice, "locking up this problem in your soul and subjecting yourself to the ridicule, disdain, and alienation of friends and family members has undermined your happiness, indeed your life. What is worse, you have not allowed justice to speak. Your wife committed a serious crime, and you have been punishing yourself for it. Is that fair? She has been leading a comfortable life while you have been leading a miserable life? Is that fair?' By the way, why didn't you confront your wife about her adultery?'

"I had no desire to hear her lies, see fake tears, or receive hypocritical promises. Honestly, I had no desire to see her. I went to America for three years, thinking that staying away from her for a while would heal my wounds, but the result was worse than I had expected. I practically consumed myself in smoking, drinking, and seducing women." Mikhail grinned sarcastically and added, "I did not care whether the woman was a stranger or a relative. My eyes were blinded to the identity of the woman I slept with. I did not care whether she was educated, illiterate, ugly, beautiful, or my neighbor's wife."

"How did your wife adjust to your new way of life?"

"At first, she was contrite and to some extent sympathetic, but then, when she felt the intensity of my contempt for her, she developed a hostile, and family members said heroic, attitude. The irony of it all is that no one knew the real reason for the change in both her and my behavior. She was certain that I did not reveal our secret only because I tried to protect my honor, and she took advantage of this fact. But unfortunately, she was the victor, I was the vanquished. A whore was treated as a saint and a saint as a villain, as a wicked person. Relatives and friends saw in her a sacrificing, devoted, and neglected wife and mother, and they saw in me a philanderer, a drunkard, and an adulterer. I have a gut feeling that my silence has created an opportunity for her to tidy her life and function as a mother but not as a neglected wife because she was proficient in the art of dissimulation. Whether in society, among friends, or in family circles, she always acted 'nicely' and refrained from saying anything inappropriate about me or anyone else. She successfully created the image of a virtuous woman and a devoted mother—"

At this point, the conversation was interrupted by the appearance of the waiter. The cousins were unaware that the restaurant had emptied and that it was time for them to leave. In fact, they were totally oblivious to the passage of time. They looked at each other with embarrassment. The waiter, who noticed their discomfort, promptly said, "Please, Mr. Jirji, you are welcome to stay here as long as you need. I have simply come to clean the tables. Would you care for some water or perhaps a glass of beer?"

"My apologies!" Jirji pleaded. "I would like a glass of cognac," Nick said.

"And your guest, Mr. Jirji, and you?"

"Some water for me," and turning his attention to Johannes, asked, "Johannes?"

"I really need some water," he hesitated a little and added, "and some cognac will be good!"

"Gladly!"

Silence reigned supreme for a few moments when the waiter left. The cousins looked at each other, their eyes and lips were silent. Nick's face was an image of somberness, of anxiety, of restlessness! He slowly turned his gaze on Johannes and said with a cynical tone in his voice, "You have said much, Johannes. One has to be a lawyer or an educated man like Jirji to be able to react intelligently to your narrative on behalf of Uncle Mikhail. I am neither a lawyer nor a university graduate. But why should I or anyone else believe the tale we have just heard? Jirji, who had assumed a deep meditative posture, fired a curious look at Nick, but the look did not linger on his face more than a second because Nick was quick to defend Aunt Rachel.

"First, no one in the family said anything bad or incriminating about Aunt Rachel now or in the past. As I pointed out earlier, she is loved and respected by the entire family. It is hard, and indeed impossible, to believe that such a woman is an adulterer or a devilish individual. Besides, she has raised two fine sons. They are highly respected by the business community, and they are regular churchgoers. Aunt Rachel taught her children to love each other, to stick together, to help one another and to live in one house even after they were married. Theirs are two families, but in fact, they are one family. Not only are they brothers, but they also raised their children as brothers and sisters. The people of Latakia speak of them with admiration and envy. Tell me, Johannes, how can anyone doubt the moral integrity of such a woman? But that is not all—" The waiter interrupted Nick's speech.

"Please, bring me the check!" Jirji said to the waiter after he placed the glasses at the table.

"It was paid."

"How?"

"By your cousin, Nadim."

"And the drinks?"

"On the house!"

"I appreciate this very much!"

When the waiter left, Nick continued:

"In contrast to Aunt Rachel, Uncle Mikhail was famous for his outrageously scandalous behavior. Show me one person in Latakia who has a high opinion of him or who respects him!"

"But," Jirji interrupted, "Uncle Mikhail admitted that he was a philanderer, a drunkard, and a seducer, that he behaved despicably, and that his wife managed to present herself to society as a virtuous woman. He also explained the reasons, of course, from his point of view, why he and his wife behaved the way they did. We may or may not blame him, we may view him as a man representing a weak or a strong character, and we may view him as a dimwit or a genius. But, based on Johannes' narrative, we cannot accuse him of deception, dishonesty, lies, or connivance. A wounded man, a man stabbed in the back, has no need to lie. Is it at all possible for a man like Oedipus the king or as Hamlet, and many Oedipuses and Hamlets now walking in the streets of our life, as they have always done in the past? Do they have to lie?"

"Oh, Jirji, I do not know much about Hamlet or Oedipus, but what baffles my mind is why he chose to hide the truth? Why did he reveal it to Johannes just before he died?"

"He answered this question during the narrative. Would you, Nick Mitya, have acted differently? Your Uncle chose to live a life of agony, of shame, and loneliness rather than be a hot item of malicious gossip and disgrace, rather than destroy the future of an innocent boy, rather than smear the honor of the Mitya family!"

"Uncle Mikhail's narrative is just a story, no more. If you wish to know the truth, all you have to do is examine your Aunt's and your Uncle's lives. What they did and how they lived should be the evidence we can rely on in our endeavor to discover the truth, not the narrative of a man dying from a bout of cancer. When the truth is revealed, when you see it with your eyes, you do not need arguments or proof. Although I do not accept Uncle Mikhail's story, I shall think about it. This is no trivial matter. But although I shall think about it, I find it hard, almost impossible, to believe the story of a despicable man."

"What do you think, Johannes?" Jirji asked. "You talked with Uncle Mikhail in great detail, and I suspect you know more than what you chose to reveal in the narrative—did he give you the impression that he was a dishonest man? Do you think that, in revealing the secret of his life to you, he was trying to repent for his sinful way of life, for the pain he inflicted upon himself, and for the countless times he embarrassed his children in public? Did he tell the truth?"

"Yes, Jirji, we talked about his life at length, we talked about the problems and the meaning of human life. Moreover, we talked about his father, for I was anxious to know as much as possible about my ancestry. I strongly believe that Uncle Mikhail did not reveal the truth about his relationship with Aunt Rachel because he felt guilty or because he was seeking redemption for his sins. The revelation of this truth, which is really tragic, formed an integral part of his recollections of his life and the history of his family. These recollections were sparked by my questions. I am profoundly interested in this subject. Frankly, I am not in a position to judge or evaluate the veracity of Uncle Mikhail's narrative primarily because I have not lived here in Latakia. But I can state with a reasonable measure of confidence that he did not lie about it. My Uncle expressed himself with the spirit of a wounded man, a man stuck in a tragic turn of events. Moreover, I did not detect any contradictions in his narrative; in fact, every word he said and every anecdote he relayed flowed from his mind spontaneously as if they happened last week. Usually, a liar hesitates when they speak, contradict themselves now and then, but not Uncle Mikhail. Just a simple question: Has anyone in the family noticed or wondered why he changed the way he treated his wife only a few years after they were married? However, Nick, one way to test the truth of Uncle Mikhail's claim is to examine the likeness, if there is any, between Abraham and Hanania and the rest of the family, even his cousins and their children."

"You are a disturber of the peace, Johannes!" Nick blurted out rather loudly. Jirji and Johannes were alarmed. They stared at him wide-eyed. "Suppose your explanation is believable, and frankly it does seem to contain the marks of believability, how can I now interact with Aunt Rachel and her children? How can the family interact with Hanania? How can Hanania interact with himself and the rest of the family? Can I treat Aunt Rachel with respect, the way I did in the past? Shall I see a bastard when I look at Hanania? If this woman is really capable of wicked behavior, what prevents me from believing that other women in the family are any different from Aunt Rachel? Moreover, how can I transform my way of regarding Aunt Rachel as a saint into seeing her as a crafty hypocrite who cannot be trusted? How would Abraham react to this information, and how would he treat his brother, Hanania? Ah, Jirji, I am confounded. Finally, should the truth about Aunt Rachel's actions be confined to us? What would our family think about Aunt Rachel's family? Would her children feel sorry for the way they treated their father? Oh, Johannes, you are a gravedigger and abuser of the dead! Yes, you must indeed be in league with the god of doubt! Did you come to Latakia to dig the graves of the Mitya family?"

Jirji embraced Nick with sympathetic eyes, so did Johannes. "I am not in league with any particular god," Johannes said. "On the contrary, I detest this god. We have no right to doubt any human being unless we are absolutely certain that they are wrong or guilty, and we cannot be certain of any claim or allegation unless our judgment is corroborated by sufficient, authoritative evidence; otherwise, we would be judging a human being unjustly—"

"We need to leave," Jirji intervened, "the waiters are preparing the tables for the evening meal. Besides, we need to be at Abraham's and Hanania's house as early as possible this evening. Why don't you accompany me to my home Johannes? You must be tired. We have a guest room. You can use it for a short respite

Johannes looked at Jirji, baffled, not because Jirji invited him to his home but because he welcomed him to his home *as a cousin."*

"Don't think about it, Johannes!" Nick said with a cordial smile. "You have no choice. This is the Mitya way."

FOUR

The Elopement of Fadya Mitya

IT WAS CUSTOMARY FOR the Mitya women to assist the wife of the family that hosts a major festive or sad event. Deema, Jirji's wife, and her child were at Rachel's house that afternoon when Johannes and Jirji arrived at the house. The rooms of the house were organized around a salon, while a reception room and a dining room were located on the northern side of the house, two bedrooms on the southern side, and a kitchen and a supply room on the northern side as well. The salon functioned as a family room. It was lined with two sofas across from each other and chairs on both sides. Jirji directed Johannes to one of the bedrooms. "This is your room," he told Johannes as he opened the door. A large bed was located in the middle of the room. It was braced by a small sofa on one side and a wardrobe on the other. "Please, feel free to lie down for a while. I shall knock at your door around five o'clock. Make yourself at home. You are home."

"Thank you, Jirji!"

Abraham and Hanania's house, which sat on four ancient groined vaults, was composed of five large bedrooms, a dining room, a supply room, a living room, a patio, and a veranda that overlooked the courtyard of the first floor. Stacks of small and large plates, silverware, and napkins were placed on the dining table in the middle of the dining room. Several young women, all dressed in black, were moving pots of cooked food from the kitchen to the dining room. The pots were sealed with covers to keep the food hot. Abraham and Hanania were standing near the entrance, welcoming the mourners to the mercy meal as they were streaming into the house.

"I would like you to meet, Johannes Mitya," Jirji said to Hanania when Jirji and his German cousin stepped onto the veranda.

"Johannes Mitya?" Hanania said in a soft, inquisitive voice.

"Yes, he is one of our cousins. He is the grandson of Hanania Mitya Sr., Uncle Mikhail's brother. He arrived in Latakia from Germany a few weeks ago." Hanania did not know how to react to this stranger.

"Welcome to our home!"

"I am pleased to meet you. Please, accept the warmest of my condolences for your loss. May your life be long and prosperous!"

"And yours!" Abraham returned. Hanania's eyes followed Jirji and Johannes as they proceeded toward the living room. Several mourners, some standing and others sitting on chairs, were socializing. Nick, who must have been waiting for his cousins, rushed to Jirji and Johannes.

"You are late! I have been waiting for you for a long time."

"Yes, we are late. I am sorry to confess that I took a long nap." This conversation was cut short by the sudden appearance of a young lady carrying a tray laden with demitasse cups of coffee. It was customary in those days to precede the mercy meal with a sip of bitter black coffee. The bitterness of the coffee symbolized the bitterness one feels of losing a loved one.

"I would like you to meet Tina Sarkisian. She is practically one of our daughters," Nick said, "and let me add that she is one of the most studious and accomplished students at the University. She won the political science award last semester."

"I am pleased to meet you!" Tina said. "Would you like a cup of coffee, Uncle Nick?" Tina asked.

"I had one, my dear, but I shall accept another one from a most beautiful lady! Who can resist a cup of coffee or—" Nick decided not to complete his sentence.

"Oh, Uncle—"

"Yes, my dear, you are the most beautiful woman in Latakia. The eyes that do not see your beauty are blind!" Tina's cheeks were covered with the most alluring blush one can see on the face of an innocent, lovely woman. Tina moved the tray forward toward Johannes and sneaked a quick but interested look at him, but his eyes were fixed on her face. Their eyes met without exchanging any pleasantries. No one will ever know what transpired during that meeting!

"Thank you!" she said after Johannes took a cup of coffee. She left a smile for Johannes' eyes to savor before returning to the kitchen.

Dressed in black like the rest of the Mitya women, Tina was, as Nick insisted, an impressively beautiful young woman. Her eyes were black and large, typical of the eyes of the beautiful Bedouin women—wild, mysterious, captivating. Although she did not apply any kind of make-up on her face, her lips were rosy and exquisite. The hands of Michelangelo must have carved them. Her face was an icon of feminine perfection. Its elegance was accentuated by a panoply of black hair. No man or woman could overlook its mystifying radiance.

The news of the arrival of the German Mitya must have spread among the cousins and their families at astonishing speed. Everyone desired to speak with him or at least take a look at his face. Nadim, who joined the Mitya men, recommended that Johannes meet Aunt Rachel as soon as possible. "She could not be ignored, not any longer!" He whispered in Jirji's ear.

Jirji and Johannes went to the living room where the women mourners were chatting and sipping black coffee. Aunt Rachel was there. "My condolences, Aunt Rachel," Jirji said to her. "May his soul rest in peace!"

"Thank you, son!"

"Allow me to introduce Johannes Mitya, grandson of Hanania Mitya." Aunt Rachel was expecting him. She directed a pointed look at Johannes's face, where it lingered for a few seconds.

"Do you know about Hanania, Aunt?" Nick, who was standing next to Jirji, asked.

"Yes, I do. He was one of Abraham's sons. He left us without saying where he was going. We never heard from him again. No one knew his whereabouts or whether he was dead or alive."

"He settled in the city of Hamburg in Germany, and he lived a good life, Aunt Rachel," Johannes said.

"You look like your grandfather. Nadim told us the story of your arrival." Aunt Rachel moved closer to Johannes and gave him a warm hug. You must stay with us. Jirji, make sure that he stays with us."

"I shall try, but I doubt that he will be able to, Aunt Rachel."

"Why not? There is more than enough space downstairs. He can occupy Uncle Mikhail's quarters."

"I shall try to convince him, Aunt."

"Have you eaten?"

"Not yet," Jirji said. "Don't worry about us. We shall eat."

"I wish to know about your family. Don't vanish the way your grandfather vanished."

"No!" Johannes replied with a pleasant smile.

"Make sure that he eats, Jirji. I should be in the kitchen now, son. I shall see you a little later."

A rapid sequence of thoughts and images coursed through Johannes's mind when Aunt Rachel left. Although his eyes were focused on his cousins, his mind was centered on the dynamic situation he found himself in. Nick's description of Aunt Rachel was mostly accurate. She spoke and conducted herself as a matriarch: caring, self-confident, and authoritative. It was clear to him, based on his brief encounter with her, that Nadim did not inform her of his intimate visits with her husband. This recognition aroused in his mind a deep feeling of satisfaction. But, did it matter to Johannes whether he or anyone else told her about the visits?

Nick was itching for a conversation with Johannes, first, to apologize to him for not believing that he was a genuine member of the family and, second, for exploring in more detail the extent of Aunt Rachel's disloyalty to her husband and whether Hanania was really a bastard. His desire to ascertain these truths was so strong, so overwhelming, it was becoming a kind of ferocious worm that began to gnaw at the walls of his mind. He had always lived with the idea that the Mityas were a pure, upstanding, and god-fearing family, a model to be emulated by the other families in Latakia. The truth that Aunt Rachel was a crafty woman and that her young son was a bastard, would undoubtedly cause visible damage to that idea, fracturing his self-esteem, dampening his pride in the Mitya family, and perhaps shaking his belief in the moral authority of the Orthodox community. It seemed that the health of his character and future happiness depended on the validity of this truth.

When such a worm scratches at the walls of the mind with its sharp teeth, it wrecks its peace and turns the scale of its priorities upside down. You slowly lose control of yourself, and you involuntarily surrender your will to your desire to know the truth. Fulfilling this desire becomes your top priority. "I hope you were able to rest a little," he said, addressing Johannes when Aunt Rachel left the four cousins, but his desire was frustrated by the sudden appearance of Jeannette. "My grandmother suggests that you begin eating your food before it gets cold," she said, and turning her face toward Johannes, continued, "she insists that you eat stuffed eggplant. This used to be my grandfather's favorite dish. You will like it!" A very soft smile danced in the corners of her mouth when she left.

"That is a good idea," Nadim said. When the four cousins entered the dining room, which was already filled with mourners, a woman in her late thirties approached Johannes. She must have just placed a big pot of food at the table. Shining drops of sweat glittered on her forehead. She pulled out a small towel stuck under the belt of her apron, dried her hands, and greeted him warmly. "I am Jameela, Hanania's wife."

Johannes was dumbfounded. He never expected to meet the woman who showed so much compassion toward Uncle Mikhail. He was speechless, but his eyes were not. They were transfixed on her ruddy face! "I have heard so much about you, and I am delighted to meet you."

"I hope you enjoy our dishes. We have been cooking Swaydieh food all morning in memory of Uncle Mikhail. Cooking this type of food is time-consuming, but it is worth it."

"I understand," Johannes said. "It is a good memory, Aunt!" Jameela allowed tears to gather in her eyes when he uttered those words; they soon rolled over her cheeks. Except for Jirji, it is doubtful whether any one of the cousins understood the meaning of those tears.

"I am delighted to meet you, Aunt Jameela," Johannes spoke warmly, appreciatively. Jameela moved closer to him and gave him a tight hug and whispered, "Don't mind my smell."

"Oh, no!" He said.

"I hope you enjoy your supper. You should pay us a visit as soon as you can!"

"I shall! The aroma has already spread throughout the house! It is delectable."

"She is a sweet woman," Nick remarked when Jameela left. All the cousins agreed with him. "Aunt Rachel will be offended if you do not eat stuffed eggplant," Nick continued, "and let me assure you that she will know if you have not tried it," Nick added.

The four cousins went back to the veranda after they filled their plates with an assortment of the dishes Jameela had prepared that morning.

"The stuffed grape leaves are especially delicious," Johannes remarked. "I wish to thank the hands that made them."

"And the stuffed eggplant?" Nick wondered. "This is Uncle Mikhail's favorite dish? Shouldn't you find it delicious?" It was clear to Jirji and Nadim that Nick was simply needling Johannes, and he was enjoying it.

"It, too, is delicious."

"I tend to agree with Johannes," Jirji interjected. "No one can cook the stuffed grape leaves better than Jameela."

"I was just teasing," Nick interjected.

Frankly, although it was a fumble, and although Nick was serious in needling Johannes, he was, in fact, trying to start a conversation with him, but his attempt was undercut by the advent of Jeannette with a paper cup containing araq for him. It was sent by his wife, Nora. "Would you like a drink, Uncle Nadim, and you, Uncle Jirji?"

"And Johannes?" Nadim queried.

"Of course, and you, Johannes!"

"I like the way you smile, Jeannette! I have not been in the habit of drinking araq, but tonight I shall drink araq."

The four cousins went back to their place on the veranda. "You cannot put your plates on your thighs!" Jeannette, who had just arrived with a tray loaded with araq paper cups, said. She placed the tray on the floor next to Nick's chair, sprinted to the supply room, and returned with four make-shift side-tables. Johannes could not suppress a smile of appreciation. This smile was followed by "Thank you." But it was not an ordinary "thank you" because he said it with a distinctive accent, one that singles you out as a special person. This kind of communication usually takes place at the level of silent dialogue. Only those who speak this language can understand it. Jeannette spoke this language, and she understood the import of his "thank you." It created a bond between them, one of trust and respect.

"I am delighted that you are observing this sad day with us, Johannes," Nick said, rather anxiously.

"Isn't he a Mitya?" Jeannette responded to her Uncle's observation.

"He is. But he will be one of us when we get to know him better, when he becomes an active member of the family," her father, Abraham, who had just joined the group, said. "Even I have not properly met him. As a matter of fact, Nadim, Johannes, has been the main subject of interest in the Mitya grapevine. You should introduce him to your aunts and the young people. They are desirous of meeting the German Mitya."

"Excellent idea!" Nick said.

Abraham, who had installed himself as the patriarch of his and Hanania's families, socialized with Johannes for a few minutes. He questioned him about his life and the life of his family in Germany the way a lawyer questions a defendant in a court of law, and he nodded judiciously every time Johannes answered a question. And, with the same interrogative posture of mind, he asked with a solemn frown, "Why didn't your grandfather write to us or let us know his whereabouts?"

"Uncle Abraham, my grandfather, did not know how to read and write. There were no Syrians where he lived. He was the only foreigner in the neighborhood. He, too, did not know where you and the rest of the family settled. Any means of communication in those days was a luxury for the rich, not accessible to the poor. But I can assure you that he was a hardworking man. He was proud of his family heritage and the Swaydieh heritage." Abraham pursed his lips and thrust a hard stare at his grandnephew:

"We are a tight-knit family. Some people here liken us to a clan not only because we descend from a great grandfather but because we share the same moral and religious values and, more importantly, because we stick together. Nick knows about our values more than anyone else. He is the pillar of the church." Abraham abruptly stopped and then added, "Our neighbors and friends will be leaving soon. Hanania and I need to bid them good-bye. In the meantime, get acquainted with your aunts and young cousins. I shall be back shortly."

On their way to the family room, where the women and the young people stayed, the four cousins had to cross the patio, which separated the room from the kitchen. But the patio was oddly quiet, so was the kitchen. Nick was apprehensive. The moment they approached the door to the room, they heard whispers and hisses seeping through the open window. Instead of seeing the cheerful female society of the family, they saw grave, gloomy faces! Jirji was alarmed. He rushed toward his wife and spoke to her with a silent but audible look as if to ask, "What is going on?" She looked around. The whispers, hustle, and murmurs were spreading like wildfire throughout the room. Deema's lips trembled. She tried to speak but was unable to utter a word. She composed herself, cleared her throat, and said, "Let us go to the patio. Nick's oldest daughter, Fadya, eloped with a Durzi man two days ago!"

"Two days ago?" Jirji exclaimed with fury in his eyes. "Did anyone know about it?"

"Her sister, Najwa. But she said nothing to anyone."

"Why?"

"She decided to wait until Uncle Mikhail was buried. She informed her mother of what happened a few minutes ago. Nora is very distressed, she is crying and does not know what to say or do. In fact, she is a nervous wreck. What is worse, she is worried about Nick. She is afraid he might do something foolish. You know your cousin! He is unpredictable!"

"Does anyone know where Fadya is? Can anyone speak with her?"

"No one knows where she is. The only thing Najwa knows is that Fadya and her husband are not in Latakia."

"Married? Husband? Is she already married? So soon?"

"That is what Najwa said."

"How does she know?

"Fadya must have revealed her plan of elopement to Najwa just before she left the house." Jirji looked at his wife, too astonished to speak.

"I think, Jirji, you should speak with Nick immediately. You know how he feels about elopement and non-Christians, Catholics, and Protestants. He will be devastated. No one will dare relay this news to him. Find a way to take him out of the room right now." Deema said and returned to the family room.

Jeannette was introducing her German cousin to her mother and the other women when Jirji signaled to Nick with a wink to join him on the patio. The mere glance *at that* signal meant, as it always did, that something serious, indeed grave, has happened. He responded to the wink with a nod and said to Tina, with whom he was talking, that he would resume their conversation momentarily. Then he proceeded to Aunt Rachel. She was sitting on the sofa, absorbed in a serious discussion with her two in-laws. "I need to leave Aunt Rachel," Nick said to the women of the house. Please accept the warmest of my condolences. May you live long!"

"May God be with you!" Rachel responded.

"That was a long day!" Nick said when he joined Jirji in the patio.

"It was long for all of us," Jirji replied. "Wait a second. I need to have a word to Nadim."

"Please, call the Schuman's and tell them that Johannes will be spending the night with me," he said to Nadim. "Try to conclude your visit here as soon as you can. Of course, bring Johannes with you—"

"Anything wrong?" Nadim interrupted Jirji.

"You will know before you leave this gathering." Jirji almost tripped at the threshold when he was leaving the room. The news of his niece's elopement was hard to believe and harder to comprehend. Alas, has the Absurd decided to pay a visit to the Mitya family? But, would this sinister power pay such a visit without a good reason? The sudden appearance of a German cousin, the revelation that Aunt Rachel was neither honest nor decent, the fact that Hanania was a bastard, the death of the oldest member of the family in Latakia, and now the elopement of Nick's oldest daughter loomed like a Greek tragedy unfolding in Jirji's consciousness. The mere perception of this drama sent shivers of fear, anxiety, and presentiment into his mind. But the story of Fadya's elopement, which was in its beginning, and Jirji would say in its middle, constrained his attention. Fadya eloped because she was happy, but Nick and his wife were miserable because she eloped! Fadya's happiness was supposed to be a source of their happiness, but now it is a source of their misery. Is this an irony of the Absurd? How should they deal with this unexpected, unimaginable turn of events?

Nick was descending the stairs when Jirji joined him. "What is going on, Jirji? Tell me!" Nick said as he was getting into Jirji's car.

"Something unpleasant happened two days ago. I would like to tell you about it."

"What is it?"

"When we arrive at home."

"Why not now? Speak! I am not a child. I can take any kind of news and any kind of setback."

"I know this and much more," Jirji said in an attempt to stall for time. Luckily, the streets were practically deserted. This provided Jirji with the opportunity to speed, and he did. His wife, Deema, was already at the house. She had to leave Abraham and Hanania's home early to bathe her child and put her to bed.

"Welcome, Nick!" she said when her husband and Nick secluded themselves in the bedroom. She knew that he was still unaware of his daughter's elopement. Accordingly, she tried to express her feeling of concern and solidarity with him, but Nick was not in a mood to listen to her or anybody else. He was mired in a thick puddle of suspense. Deema noticed his mood and respected his wishes. She went to the kitchen and debated whether to brew a cup of coffee.

"What is going on, Jirji? For god's sake, tell me!"

"Strange things happen in our lives, Nick—"

"Don't beat around the bush! Get straight to the point." Nick said with undeniable irritation.

"Allow a storm to burst. Let it rage, let it rumble, and let it wreak all the havoc it can wreak since no one can change its course, diffuse it, or stop it. Then do all you can to control the damage it leaves behind. Human beings can control their ideas, feelings, and emotions, but they cannot control what befalls them by nature and the actions of others." This piece of Stoic wisdom, which was repeatedly emphasized by one of Jirji's professors when he was in the seminary, flashed through his consciousness that evening. It illuminated his mind when Nick pressed him to speak. It is strange that most of the time, we do not truly understand the scientific, philosophical, and artistic concepts and principles we study in school until we *think of them in context*, that is, when a given situation calls for or reveals their meaning or relevance. The power that reveals this meaning or significance is the power of reason. We see the situation through the eyes of those concepts and principles, enabling us to intuit, conceive, understand or evaluate the situation. Jirji knew that the task he was about to perform was one of "damage control" to help Nick first comprehend what happened and then help him to deal with it rationally, if possible. We cannot resurrect past events in the sphere of the present, but we can learn from them, although people rarely do. Do we not feel enlightened about ourselves and others when we make mistakes, when we witness the errors of others, or when we watch others suffer from natural evils such as earthquakes, disease, or floods? But, then, how should Jirji begin the process of damage control? *Tell the truth!* How do we manage the damage if we do not know its nature and cause? The truth may be painful, but the pain will be higher, now or later, if we evade or veil it, and it will be less if we communicate it in the right way—compassionately, supportively, and generously. This is what Jirji did. With sympathetic eyes and a palpitating heart, he said:

"Your daughter, Fadya, eloped with a young Durzi man two days ago—"

"What? My daughter eloped with a Durzi two days ago? Are you out of your mind, Jirji? My daughter, Fadya?" Nick exploded.

"Yes!"

"Impossible!"

"Many of the things which seem impossible in our lives are possible. This is one of them."

"Impossible! Not my daughter! She never missed liturgy. She always fasted and made everyone in the family fast. She was an exemplary daughter of the church. Neither I nor anyone in this world can believe that she would elope with a Durzi. Besides, Jirji, how can she even form a relationship with a person who is practically a Muslim? No, not my daughter! She would at least confide in her mother, but she never did." Nick was so emotional, he could not think! He paused for a second and almost shouted, "A Durzi?

Oh, no! How can she elope with such a man?" He shook his head several times and suddenly fell silent for a few seconds. He stared at the ground as if he was looking for some kind of revelation or some spirit that would agree with him. "Did she make the decision herself, or was she seduced by a lustful, cunning charlatan?" He cried after he extricated himself from that stare. "No Jirji! How can she deprive her mother and the entire family of the joy of planning her wedding and witnessing it? How can she deprive us of the pleasure of celebrating her transition into womanhood? Is this true, Jirji?"

"It is true," Jirji said in a very soft voice.

"It cannot be a fact, because it is impossible! The impossible can never be a fact!"

"All facts are possible, otherwise, they would not be facts. It is a fact; therefore, it is possible, therefore, believable."

"Even if it is a fact, it is not believable. How can it be, if it is against the sacred values, traditions, and beliefs of our life, of the church? It is even against the laws of nature!"

"The laws of nature are different from the laws of our humanity. The former are necessary, while the latter are not." Jirji said in the same soft voice.

"Oh, Jirji, how can she marry a man who is not baptized by an Orthodox priest?" Nick stopped, peered through the dark window with delirious eyes. He was exhausted. He thrust a confused but sad look at Jirji and said,

"By the way, who spread this rumor?"

"It is not a rumor. It is a fact. Fadya communicated her plan to Najwa and insisted that she tell her mother about it after Uncle Mikhail was buried."

"My daughter, Najwa? And she kept this secret until now?"

"Najwa had no choice. She meant well. She is crushed by Fadya's elopement. She has not stopped crying since her sister left the house—"

"I shall deal with her later."

"No, Nick, you cannot deal with her now or later. She, her mother, and everyone in the family are in smoldering torment over this. Enough punishment! Enough pain! Najwa is in burning agony—isn't this more than enough punishment?"

Nick sank into a frightful spell of silence. It seemed that his eyes, his lips, even his hands were frozen. At first, Jirji did not take this abrupt transformation seriously, for he thought that his cousin was trying to collect his thoughts and emotions, but that was not the case, because he lingered in that frozen state for a long moment. Jirji was frightened. He could not speculate about Nick's emotional state or the ideas that were coursing through his mind or perhaps clouding his vision. He knew that Nick was devastated. He also knew that he was impulsive. A man in his condition can act irrationally. But luckily, Nick spoke!

"Jirji," he said with a sardonic smile quivering at the corners of his mouth, "look at this scandal—and yes, it is a scandal—in its wider context, not as an event that can be locked in a drawer or shoved under the rug. Frankly, if what you have just told me is true, let it be. I do not wish to see Fadya again, but if I see her, *I shall kill her*. From now on, I do not have a daughter called Fadya!"

"You will not kill her because you are not a killer. A loving father is a loving human being, and a loving human being cannot ordinarily kill another human being. A son of the church can never be a killer. *Be yourself.* Fadya is your daughter, and she will always be your daughter—"

"Oh, Jirji," Nick said, "you are out of place in this world! You belong in a monastery or some kind of hermitage—"

"Nick!"

"Don't Nick me! Look at the ramifications of this scandal. You see, it does not impact only my wife, me, and my children but the whole Mitya family. What will the people say about us—great examples of the church? Is this the kind of example you wish to portray to your friends and neighbors? Did Fadya think of us as a family or only of her selfish pleasure? Is this how she repays her parents? Is this her 'thank you' to them, to this entire family? How can I face the priest, the Sabas, and every family in the church? How can I even dare go to the church? What kind of lesson has Fadya given to her sister, cousins, and brothers? Where did all this Christian teaching go—to a Durzi?

"I am worried about my wife more than my children or me. The fingers of all the men and women of the church will point at her as a bad mother: how can she look them in the eye? How can she be a proud mother? Doesn't a good mother have a right to be proud of her children? Has it occurred to you that marrying a Durzi without the knowledge and approval of her parents means a total rejection of the values and traditions of the church and our family? By marrying a Durzi, Fadya has pulled out her religious and cultural roots from the soil that nourished her from the moment she was born to the present. This is tantamount to a chilling act of self-abnegation—of burying her true self and growing a new one in different soil.

How can you say that she will remain my daughter? What is the basis of 'my' in 'my daughter' but the beliefs and values we share? Will she remain, my daughter, if she grows new beliefs and values in a different cultural and religious soil? How can she utter the word 'father' or 'daughter' anymore?

"What is even worse, Jirji is that in choosing a Durzi as her husband, she will necessarily alienate herself from her family, friends, neighbors, as well as her true happiness. Think of this whole matter from the perspective of her lover's parents, if he is a true lover—will they accept her as one of them? Suppose they accept her as his wife, will they accept her as a Christian wife? Ah! How do we know that he is a true lover? Suppose he satiates his sexual desire with her and then feels bored with her, what then? What if she is pregnant when he dumps her?" Nick's right hand trembled a little, and then he froze the way he froze a short while ago but not for long. He shook his head sideways with the same sardonic smirk in the corners of his mouth. Nick was frightened, not of Jirji or anybody in the family or society but of himself. His fear crept into his eyes. His startled eyes fired a concerned look at Jirji, but it was shattered by the sudden appearance of Deema. She first knocked at the door and then opened it. Two cups of coffee rattled on a brass tray as she moved closer to the two cousins. Nick was seated in an armchair near the bed, and Jirji was sitting at its edge.

"The whole family knows about the elopement, Nick," Deema said. "Frankly, they are more worried about you than about Fadya. They know how you feel about marriage and the family. Ironically, your daughter is happy with her elopement, and you are miserable with it. Let me assure you that no one in the Mitya family is pleased with what happened. They sympathize with you and your wife. But it is useless to cry over spilled milk." Deema hesitated a little and continued, "I have a strong feeling that things will be fine, Nick. Fadya is a good woman. She loves you, and if you allow me to express my opinion," which she did anyway, "I can say she adores you and your wife. Nothing in the world can shake her love for you." The fury that was flaming in Nick's mind did not subside but receded a little from his consciousness. He stared at his sister-in-law with puzzled eyes. Deema could not decipher the message of his gaze. "Nadim and Johannes are in the living room," she continued. "They arrived an hour ago. Would you like to join them?" she asked, still carrying the brass tray in her hands.

"Of course," Jirji retorted and then, turning his face toward Nick, said, "it is good for Nadim and Johannes to take part in this conversation. What do you think?" Nick, who was still struggling with that flame of fury, responded with a nod of approval.

The cousins took their coffee cups from the brass tray on their way out of the bedroom. Nick's face was oozing gloom. The idea that his oldest daughter eloped with a Durzi had not yet sunk in. "I hope you had a chance to meet all the members of the family," Jirji asked Johannes.

"Yes, I did. I also met Armen, Tina's mother; she is a fine woman. I had a fascinating conversation with Yuri on the similarities and differences between the German and Syrian systems of university education. The Syrian department of education seems to follow in the footsteps of the American system. I was very pleased, in fact, surprised to discover that Tina is a political science major. She raised several important questions about the nature of government, law, justice, and freedom. She is a very bright woman and commands the central questions of political science. Her remarks about these questions were provocative and, in fact, intriguing. I look forward to discussing them in detail with her in the near future."

"Next Sunday," Nadim interjected. "Her mother invited him to have supper with them on Sunday."

"You are being initiated into the Mitya family smoothly," Jirji remarked.

"Why not?" Nick remarked with obvious sarcasm in his voice. "He is a most eligible bachelor—"

"Nick!" Jirji interrupted. "Don't go too far. The man has just arrived in Latakia. He did not come to find a wife but to do research on a serious academic project. I doubt that he will have time to flirt with women or marry one." Nick chuckled with the same sarcastic tone in his voice.

"Thank you, Jirji," Johannes interjected.

"Are you sure, cousin?" Nick asked Jirji.

"I am. Academic research is time-consuming; it requires focus, diligence, and dedication."

"But he is a man, therefore, he has a man's needs. Can he or any other man ignore these needs? Many of the goals we pursue and the projects we undertake in our lives fall within the parameters of some kind of law, norm, tradition, rule, or custom, but the monster people call love does not follow any law, rule, custom, tradition, or custom. He is a wild, capricious animal that roams the jungle of human society. Look at my saintly daughter, Fadya. Who could have predicted that she would fall in love with a Durzi? Who could have thought that this loving and lovable young woman would renounce her parents, family, traditions, and all the laws of our culture for love—of course, if the story of her elopement happens to be true." Nick said the last few words with emphasis.

"The elopement is a fact, Nick, and it is a depressing fact," Nadim said. "All the members of the family know about it and treat it as a fact. If it is not, and you still seem to be in denial about it, why isn't she here? Why has she missed the funeral? It is bizarre that the whole family knows this as a fact, but not you! Besides," Nadim pressed on, "why can't you believe that your daughter fell in love with a Durzi if, as you said, love is a wild, capricious animal?"

"Saying that love is a wild animal is one thing, and eloping with a Durzi is something else."

"Why is it something else? Is a Durzi not a human being? Was he not created by the god you worship? Is he not made of the same stuff every human being is made of?"

"But he is different."

"How?"

"He is a Durzi!"

"Do you mean his religion is different?"

"Yes."

"What is wrong with marrying a Durzi?"

"Durzis are different people."

"They are different by virtue being Durzis, right?"

"Yes."

"But Durzis worship the same God Christians worship. They worship him differently. Don't Catholics, Protestants, and the Orthodox faithful, who are Christians, worship God differently?"

"Yes."

"Don't the different Orthodox churches in the different parts of the world also worship God differently? Does it matter how we worship God as long as we worship Him?"

"Yes, it matters. If you worship God the Christian way, you are a Christian, and if you worship Him the Durzi way, you are a Durzi. A Durzi thinks, feels, and acts according to the beliefs and values of the Durzi way of life. Their way of life is different from ours."

"But does it really matter if one worships God in any particular way?"

"It matters significantly!"

"How?"

"If you think, feel, and act as a Durzi, your worldview is different. How can two people with two different ways of life live harmoniously or even love each other? How can they be happy when their beliefs, tastes, habits, desires, values, and the way they understand the meaning of human life are different? Can they love each other if they do not share their lives? But how can they share their lives if they are different?"

"They can love each other because they are human beings. Love is a human need. It is always aimed at another human being. Love is blind; it does not see color, wealth, or social status; it does not see whether you are short or tall, teacher or farmer, soldier or businessperson, politician or priest, or whether you have brown or blue eyes, dark or blond hair. Is loving and being loved not the highest aim of the lover? Don't you think that a Durzi, a Hindu, or a Jew, can love as beautifully and as profoundly as a Christian can?"

"Yes."

"But, if two people love each other, don't you think they can chart a harmonious way of living?"

"I doubt it. They have to change their way of thinking, feeling, and acting first. This is not easy."

"But no two people, regardless of their family, social, professional, or cultural affiliation, think, feel, and act in the same way. It takes time for any two human beings, regardless of their religion, to get used to each other, to accept each other as they are, and to build a harmonious way of living. Would you agree?"

"But it seems to me, cousin, that the real issue we have to endow with serious consideration is whether the man or the woman is a good human being."

"What do you mean?"

"Would you like your daughter to marry a bad Christian man or a good Christian man?"

"That is a strange question."

"Maybe. Is a good person necessarily a good person merely because he is Christian, Jew, Hindu, or Durzi? Isn't it possible for a Christian to be a bad human being?"

"Of course, Uncle Mikhail is a good example."

"It should follow that you would like your daughter to fall in love with not merely with a Christian man but with a good Christian man—would you agree?"

"Yes.

"What matters, then, is goodness—would you agree?"

"Yes."

"Now, is it possible for a non-Christian person to be a good person? What makes a Christian person a good person? Before you answer my question, survey in your mind the different non-Christian people you know in Latakia. Are some of them good?" Nick pierced a tense look into Jirji's eyes and with a cynical smirk on his lips said:

"You must be a wizard!"

"A wizard? This is a new kind of characterization of me, Nick! Why am I a wizard?"

"Because I am absolutely confident that the Orthodox brand of Christianity is the true religion. Nobody and nothing in this world can change this fact, and it is a fact, Jirji. More than anyone in this family, you should be familiar with this particular truth. You are trying to make me change my mind." Jirji smiled and said:

"You are hasty."

"Am I?"

"Yes."

"But we should not digress from the main topic of this conversation— don't you think?"

"Yes," Nick said. "You are trying to change my way of thinking about Durzi people, but you will not succeed."

"It is doubtful that this is my purpose. No one can force you to change your mind about your basic beliefs. The only thing that inclines us to change the way we think or feel is the combined powers of will and a rational vision of the truth. A person has to discern the truth of an idea, comprehend it, and accept it willingly. But, again, we should not lose sight of the question at hand. Do you think that a non-Christian can be a good person?"

"Honestly, I have met some Muslims, Jews, and Alawites who are not only good people but also better than many of the Orthodox people who go to church on Sunday."

"Excellent! Then, the real problem that glares us in the face is the source or basis of goodness: if a Christian or non-Christian can be good, what makes them a good human being? Can a Christian misbehave and remain a true Christian? What about the Christian or non-Christian that makes them a good human being? Now, would you agree that a good Christian lives according to the beliefs and values of the Christian church?"

"Yes."

"Accordingly, a person who acts contrary to them would be a bad person. Here, we assume that we know whether a person is good or bad by examining their actions. They are good if they instantiate them, bad if they are contrary to them. Would you agree?"

"Yes."

"What are the values that define goodness?"

"This is the crux of the question that troubles me: How can a Christian and a Durzi be alike in their conception of goodness and differ in their conception of religion?"

"Because there are two types of beliefs and values, the first defines religious behavior and life, the second defines moral behavior and life. The first expresses a community's understanding of God and the relation that exists between God and human beings and the second expresses the nature of the moral life. The first shows people how to worship and glorify God, while the second shows them how they should live. This manifold distinction reveals two dimensions of values, namely religious and moral. The religious dimension is concerned with the immortality of the soul, last judgment, heaven and hell, and the impulse to know and have union with God. Christians and Muslims believe in the immortality of the soul, heaven and hell, and last judgment. They also believe that God, who is a transcendent being, created the universe and humanity, and revealed himself to human beings, but differently. While Jesus is the instrument of this in Christianity, Muhammad is the instrument of revelation in Islam. How God revealed himself to human beings, as well as the content of this revelation, has been the subject of extensive study by theologians over the past sixteen hundred years. We should steer away from this topic and emphasize that the main concerns of Muslims and Christians are heaven and hell, the immortality of the soul, the absoluteness of God, and the obligation to live according to the truth revealed in their revelations. Following the teaching of one of these religions does not only define religiosity but also moral goodness. A person is religious since they live according to the religious beliefs and values of their religion, while they are moral since they live according to the moral values of their religion. The question which seems to trouble you is the source and identity of these values—correct?"

"Yes."

"Let us now ask: what are these values? These values are usually called virtues. Broadly speaking, we can say that they are justice, compassion, love," friendship, honesty, courage, respect for the person and property of other human beings, humility, faith, mercy, keeping promises, and related values. Each one of these virtues is a moral value, and each moral value functions as a basis, or a standard, for acting in a certain way. For example, an action that conforms to the standard of justice would be viewed as a moral action, one that is performed contrary to it would be viewed as an immoral action. The unity of these values constitutes the morality of a community, and their unity in the character of the individual constitutes their moral character. Has it occurred to you, dear Nick, that Muslims and Christians practically espouse similar conceptions of moral goodness? As you can see, what matters in real life is goodness."

"If what matters in real life is moral goodness, what is the use of religiosity, of being Christian or Muslim, or Hindu?"

"Your question is a logical consequence of my emphasis on the supreme importance of moral goodness in our lives. Let me confess that the question you raised cannot be analyzed in detail in the present conversation primarily because it implies the discussion of a plethora of very recalcitrant questions—"

"But how can the discussion of moral goodness be useful to me in my miserable condition if you do not explain the relationship between the religious and the moral? I repudiate the elopement of my daughter with a Durzi mainly because he is a Durzi. Being a good man, supposing that he is good, is important, but it is not enough for me. I am now convinced more than ever before that not only Christians but also non-Christians can be good human beings and should be respected and admired when they act morally. My daughter has eloped with a Durzi and maybe with a good man. If religion is a way of life, moral behavior is only a part of it. Can we understand the way a Durzi is a good man if we do not also understand the way he is a religious man?"

"This is a fair question, but I will answer it on one condition."

"What is it?"

"The question you raised is enmeshed in a dense and complicated thicket of theological views and controversies, which is unwise even to broach in this conversation, but I shall be happy to make some important remarks based on my own reflections. Would that be agreeable to you?"

"You can neither shrink nor retreat from voicing your opinion on the relation between religion and moral goodness. Frankly, I would not understand these views and controversies even if you tried to present them to me. Your remarks, Jirji, will be enough for me!"

"You are generous, Nick! A person who has been listening to our conversation carefully would, I think, wonder: Why would the different religions of the world, even communities that do not advocate a certain religion, prize the values that make up the concept of moral goodness? People do not uphold them only as the defining features of moral goodness; they also feel that they should act according to them. For example, 'Love your fellow human being! Tell the truth! Be courageous!' are not merely recommendations for a particular type of behavior; they are also obligations. What is the source of this obligation? If in a situation of love, truth-telling, or courage, I act selfishly, dishonestly, or cowardly, I feel guilty. Why should I feel guilty? I am not, in raising this question, looking for a psychological, social, or biological explanation but instead for a philosophically compelling, justifiable explanation.

"We may argue that moral values are intrinsically valuable, that is, they do not derive their validity from the state, society, an individual, natural impulse or from some external power but from the value that inheres in them. They are good in themselves, not as a means to an external end, for example, advantage. Their value forms part of their essential nature. We may also say that what is essentially important to us as human beings is a justifiable source of the obligation. Therefore, acting honestly or courageously from a sense of moral obligation is justifiable because honesty and courage are intrinsically valuable."

"But," Johannes, who has been quiet so far, intervened, "would all thinkers in the different religions, as well as the faithful, agree to this type of explanation?"

"No, I appeal to it only because some of the major philosophers endorsed it. But regardless of whether a universally accepted explanation exists or will exist in the near or distant future, the question that merits our special attention is this: Let us grant for the sake of discussion that goodness is intrinsically valuable, still, why should I act according to its precepts?"

"I agree with you, Jirji," Nick intervened, "parents, teachers, philosophers, priests, and ordinary people have been saying, ever since the dawn of Western Civilization, that we should act morally. They praise moral action, they respect and admire the moral character and try their best to convince the young people to act morally, even though most of the time they do not act morally, why? Why should I act morally? Why do people pursue their personal advantage rather than good? Why do they wear the mask of moral goodness and carry its banner in public, but in fact, they advance their personal interests? Don't they use the mask of moral goodness as a means to an end, and the end is personal advantage? Don't they repudiate the validity of the claim that moral goodness is a standard of human excellence, by their action? What is the use of a standard of human excellence that does not promote personal advantage?"

"But," Johannes said, "there were, and always will be, people like Socrates, who are willing to sacrifice their lives for the sake of moral goodness. How many a social leader, a revolutionary, a nurse, a teacher, or a soldier died for the sake of moral goodness, or for the sake of a moral cause? How many a human being preferred to suffer the pangs of injustice, of poverty, of discrimination, of social alienation, and of ridicule, rather than trample on the precepts of moral goodness? Doesn't this show, at least to some extent, that moral goodness is worth dying for? What is the difference between surviving as a selfish human being and dying as a noble person? Can we say that the person who died for the noble cause lived a less worthwhile life than the one who remained in their selfish dungeon?"

"We may agree or disagree on whether moral goodness is worth dying for," Jirji said. "For example, luminaries such as Aristotle chose not to die for the sake of the good and preferred to live, saying that he would not let those who were planning to kill him, sin twice against philosophy. Is this line of reasoning valid? But what intrigues me is whether moral goodness is intrinsically valuable and a justifiable source of moral obligation. I tend to think that it is not."

"Why?" Johannes asked.

"The concept of intrinsicality does not logically entail any kind of obligation. Good may be intrinsically valuable without necessarily being obligatory. It can be pursued for personal advantage. For example, knowledge is good, but we frequently seek it as a means to an individual or collective advantage. We can choose not to seek knowledge with impunity. But can we choose to act selfishly with impunity? No. Intrinsicality is not enough. There must be something special about moral goodness that makes it a source of moral obligation. I am not unaware of the grand and admirable attempts of the philosophers to advance an absolutely valid justification for moral goodness as a source of obligation, one that commands universal assent. These attempts were, and will always originate from a particular philosophical, cultural, or religious ideology or worldview. The rational, as one German philosopher pointed out, is real, but the real is an on-going process of change and development. Compare the works of reason today to those of five thousand or two thousand years ago, and then continue gradually until today. Reason is power, and the sphere of influence of this power continues to grow and develop in the different areas of human experience and inquiry.

"You see, Johannes, and you too, Nick, regardless of its level of perfection, the human mind always thinks and justifies its beliefs from its perspective. But this perspective is an on-going process of change. It can no more transcend its powers of perception and cognition than a human being can leap over the Atlantic Ocean. But, let me remind you that the human mind is not a perfect faculty. It is finite and will always be finite. It may grow in perfection, but it will never be perfect. It may have supremely noble visions of moral values, and it may create sophisticated methods for establishing their importance and utility, but these methods will always fall short of perfection. It can never be a source of absolute certainty of our beliefs in any theoretical or practical domain of our lives. A measure of faith, of commitment, regardless of whether it is strong or weak, underlies our beliefs and our life-projects in the areas of science, philosophy, art, and practical life. Broadly speaking, this faith originates from a pragmatic need to continue with the development of our personal scientific and artistic endeavors. It is, I think, an indispensable condition for our *human* as well as *biological* survival. Doubt is one of the important sources of anxiety. It underlies the impulse to inquire, to wonder, and in some cases to hope, but it can also stultify this impulse. The most important power that can transform it into a constructive force is faith, not any kind of faith, but the kind that originates from the depth of reason.

"This kind of faith is not idiosyncratic or blind but founded in deep contemplation on the essential nature and purpose of the amazing tapestry that makes up the structure of the cosmos and human civilization. Although we question it now and then, in different ways, and for different reasons, it is reliable, if not more reliable, than any kind of knowledge, whether theoretical or practical.

"Founding our knowledge of moral values in faith in God, in the source of the universe, can justify the obligation to live according to these requirements. I tend to think that choosing to die for them is founded in faith, in the wisdom of the power that created the universe, not as an ultimately created object but as an on-going process of creation, as a continual advance in creative vision and realization of this vision."

"Can you elaborate on this point, please?" Johannes asked.

"Regardless of the nature of the force that created the universe or the kind of relationship it has with the universe and humanity, it is reasonable to say that it is wise. I do not need to advance scientific proof of this claim. I simply invite you or anyone in this entire universe to reflect on it and discern the inner dynamics of the cosmic process. Neither you nor I will be conducting this conversation if this force is not wise, of course not in the philosophical sense of 'wise' but in the ontological sense.

"Now, if the creator of the universe is wise, and it is wise, human values that express the highest aspiration of human nature and the finest and noblest mode of being in this universe, it would be reasonable to say that attainment of these values would represent the supreme goal of the cosmic process. If these values can be the supreme goal of the cosmic process, would it be outlandish to say that it is justifiable for a human being to die for them?" Johannes allowed a deep sigh to escape from his nostrils. He frowned and regarded Jirji reflectively. Jirji, who felt the impact of this look, added, "I know that this last remark is extremely succinct. I did not make it either thoughtlessly or rashly."

"I understand the purport of this response, and I shall not request a detailed explanation of it, at least not now, but the problem that is uppermost on Nick's mind is the relation between moral values and religion. How can different accounts of the will, or word, of God be the source of the same moral values? Are they independent of each other?"

"No, they are intrinsically related to each other, and I dare say that the religious stratum is a necessary condition for the moral stratum of religion mainly because ontologically the religious is more primary than the moral. The encounter between God and the founders of the major religions is the source of religious and moral beliefs. Let me remind you here, that most of the religions view themselves as unique, as radically different from the other religions, and we can say as exclusive, but, as I pointed out earlier, they are similar in their conceptions of God and the meaning of human life and destiny. The differences are attributable to their different cultural orientations or worldviews. As a theology, or as a conceptual framework, the essential elements of every religion are written in the language of its culture at a different historical stage of human development. For example, all the religions aver that God is transcendent and ineffable, that He is the creator of the universe, and that He is the overseer of the cosmic process. Their interpretations and translations of the content of this revelation into a way of life differ from one religion to another, but regardless of this difference, they share the fundamental beliefs and values.

"I do not exaggerate if I say that the highest goal of all the religions is the ennoblement and hopefully the perfection of human nature. This is why it would be a mistake to say that 'my' religion is better than 'yours.' I am convinced that if a Durzi, a Christian, or a Jew honestly lives according to their religious, moral values and beliefs, they will be as attractive and lovable and as respectable and admirable as any other believer in their religious community.

"Imagine a circle, view this circle as an infinite depth. Then, imagine different roads leading to this circle concentrically. If you do, you can see the different faiths marching on this road toward this center and gradually toward the infinite depth. The question is not whether I am a Christian or a Durzi, but whether I am an authentic Christian or an authentic Durzi, whether the moral and religious beliefs of my religion shine through my actions the way the sun shines through its rays—"

"Are you a Christian, Jirji?" Nick asked with a shade of sarcasm in his voice. It was clear to his cousins that he was not pleased with Jirji's view of the relation between the different religions. Johannes looked at him, astonished. His look lingered on Nick's face for a few seconds. Apparently, Jirji, who understood Nick's way of thinking and feeling better than Johannes, said:

"I am a person who aspires to be a genuine Christian. I am proud to be a Christian just as a Hindu, a Durzi, or a Buddhist is proud to be a Hindu, a Durzi, or a Buddhist.

"You asked me a very significant question, Nick. I answered it to the best of my ability. I know it was brief, but it was impossible to give a detailed account in this conversation. I do not ask you to agree with me, I only ask you to think about what I said. Remember: we have not chosen to be Christians, Durzis, or Muslims. We discover ourselves as Christians, Durzis, and Muslims later on when we become conscious of our personal and cultural identity. Did anyone ask you whether you wanted to be born in any particular family, religion, or society? What gives me the right to say that my religion is better than yours? Has it occurred to you that most of the faithful in the different religions do not know the theology of their own religion and that they are certainly ignorant of the theology of the other religions, and yet they hate or disapprove of the other religions? How can we love or hate anything without the knowledge of what we love and hate? Why? This is a sad state of affairs—"

The eyes of the cousins abruptly gravitated toward Deema's figure that stood behind her husband's chair. She graced them with a soft smile. She was dressed in her evening gown. Although she did not make any comment, her presence signified that it was time to end the conversation. Every one of the cousins reflexively looked at his watch. "Oh, goodness!" Nadim said. "It is time to go. But before I leave, let me tell you, Jirji, that I was deeply impressed by your answer to Nick's question. You have provoked me to re-think some of my ideas about Christianity and especially about religion. What you said tonight was succinct. Can we have another conversation on this topic, if possible?"

"That is an excellent proposal!" Johannes said in support of Nadim's request," and turning his face toward Jirji, added, "you have no choice! Three against one!"

"I shall be happy to converse with you on this subject."

FIVE

Bassam Mitya Commits a Capital Crime

ON THE FOLLOWING SUNDAY, when liturgy was over, and several members of the faithful gathered, as usual, in the courtyard of the church and gossiped and reviewed the news of the week, Jirji, who had brought Johannes from Bouqa that morning to celebrate Holy Communion with the family, approached Yuri Sarkisian, Armen's husband, and introduced him to his German cousin. "We have met and discussed the state of education in Germany and Syria. I have heard many good things about you," Yuri said to Johannes.

"I hope," Johannes said with a feeling of embarrassment. For some reason, Johannes did not feel comfortable with any kind of compliment.

"My wife told me that Jirji has already given you a grand tour of the city of Latakia and its environs."

"It was a grand tour, indeed. It was a delightful, informative, and meaningful experience. I never thought that a rich history thrives in this quiet part of Syria. One can feel the spirit of Greek and Roman civilizations reverberating in its streets, in its mountains, and in its shoreline. I am looking forward to visiting the other cities, museums, and historical sites of Syria in the near future—"

"This German cousin is a rabble-rouser, Yuri," Nick, who was chatting with a friend next to Yuri, said. "He and Jirji are wizards. They can make you believe that you exist and don't exist at the same time and in the same place, and they can change your belief about God, the church, and the immortality of the soul without even knowing that you have changed it. Please, be very careful with this duo!" And then, turning his face toward Jirji, continued,

"You cannot extricate yourself unscathed from the obligation to shed more light on the relation between religion and moral goodness."

"We can continue this conversation at my house this afternoon," Yuri said. He put his hand on Nick's shoulder and led the group to his house, which was within walking distance from the church.

The Mitya and Sarkisian women did not attend liturgy that morning. They had to wait at least thirty days before they could visit anyone or take part in social events or even take a walk on the cornice on Sunday afternoon. Respect for the dead was a sacrosanct norm in the Mitya family. Aunt Rachel enforced this norm with a seriously religious spirit. For her, tradition was as sacred as the rules, norms, and practices of the church. But she made an exception that Sunday. She allowed her granddaughter, Jeannette, to help Armen and her aunts in the kitchen that Sunday. It seemed to some of her grandchildren and grandnephews that Aunt Rachel's instructions were extensions of the Holy Writ. It was difficult for anyone to doubt or question any aspect of the family or church tradition.

Tina was arranging the plates on the dining room table when she heard her father's customary knock at the front door. She left them where they were, and rushed to the door. Five men filed into the house the way soldiers enter a mess hall after a hard day's training. "Dinner will be served in about an hour," she said after she had welcomed the Mitya men to her home.

"We came a bit early," Nadim remarked.

"Oh, no, Uncle Nadim," she said, "you can never be early or late at your home!" Nadim moved closer to her and hugged her warmly.

"Why don't you enjoy a light drink in the meantime?" she said to the men who were blessed by the spirit of the Holy Communion and then, with a charming smile, added, "You too, Johannes, can enjoy a glass of the araq my father has made. But I warn you, it is very strong!"

What young man in the prime of his youth can resist the smile of a beautiful woman? Beauty is attractive, but when it is baptized with the hands of a good heart and the spirit of a lucid mind, it is captivating. It was difficult to judge whether Tina's warm welcome to Johannes was intended to impress the German visitor or simply to make him feel at home. An objective observer would have said that she was her true self. Indeed, no one of the Mitya cousins found her welcome unusual. Nonetheless, it impressed Johannes differently, not because he was the doubting kind, not because the welcome was warm, but because it was truly charming. He felt the charm, he enjoyed it, and he allowed it to flow freely into his mind.

"Johannes can drink better than anyone of us, my dear," Nick, who was always ready to drive a spike into Johannes's side, said, "he is not a weakling. He has a big heart in his chest and a bigger mind on his shoulders! Just wait until you know him better. He is a mind twister. I am sure he and Jirji can make you believe in the goodness of the devil, although it is stated in the bible that the devil is the source of all the evil in the world. Tina stared at Nick, the look in her eyes inquisitive. Nick understood the meaning of the stare. "You should have heard Jirji, with Johannes at his side, prove to me and Nadim that the Durzi version of God's revelation is as valid as the Christian version, that their moral values are essentially similar to ours, and that their religious way of life as good as ours, therefore, it is perfectly fine for my daughter to elope with a Durzi man. If members of the church heard his views on divine revelation, moral goodness, the relation between religion and morality, they would think he is an atheist and certainly a blasphemer."

"Why don't you move to the living room, Uncle Nick?" Tina suggested with a friendly voice. "I would very much like to listen to your discussion of any aspect of religion. I am anxious to see how Jirji and Johannes practice their wizardry." Yuri moved closer to Tina and kissed her on the head. He loved his daughter profoundly.

Soon after the men were seated in the living room, Armen, accompanied by Sarah, Nadim's wife, and Jeannette, walked in. Their faces were ruddy and a little sweaty. They were cooking the Sunday dinner. Nora, Nick's wife, who desired to spend the day with the Sarkisians, could not come only because she had to tend to her sick father. "Bien Venue!" Armen said to her guests. She taught French at Joul Jammal High School and frequently expressed herself in French. She turned her face toward Johannes and said, "Welcome to our home!"

"I am very pleased to be invited to your home. In fact, I have been looking forward to this visit."

"I hope we do not disappoint you!"

"Not at all! I am confident it will be a wonderful day for my cousins and me."

"Here goes Cupid!" Nick whispered in Nadim's ear. "Cupid is about to shoot his arrow." Nadim bit his lower lip and stepped on Nick's foot. "Stop it," he whispered back.

The ladies returned to the kitchen after they exchanged a few pleasant-ries with the men. Although he did not admit it, not even to his wife, Nick wished that his son, Faris, would marry Tina. It was time for him to stop being a Casanova and get settled. The mere look at Tina aroused a strong desire in him to have grandchildren from Tina and his oldest son. Besides, Tina was not only beautiful, but she was also chaste. Chasity in women, not men, was a supreme value for the Mitya family; it was a necessary condition for marriage. For them, it was a clear indication of virtue! Chastity was more, much more, superior to honesty, justice, love, courage, or wisdom. Nick wanted to make an overture, at least a hint, at the right time and in the most appropriate way, to Tina directly or to her father that it was good for Tina and Faris to be engaged. But he was not a very diplomatic man, and he knew it! He simply did not wish to botch this possibility, so he decided to bide his time and wait for the right opportunity to make his move.

The echo of Nick's desire, which was crawling in his mind like a cutworm, reached his wife's ears. The realization that Johannes was an eli-gible bachelor and the warm reception he received at the Sarkisian house aroused a feeling of jealousy in her heart. Like her husband, Nora had been hoping, for more than a year, that her son would "one day" marry Tina. But, alas, this attractive and highly educated German Mitya stood before her eyes as formidable competition for her son. The urgency of the feeling she, like her husband, was having that morning converted the "one-day" idea into "now." Parents cannot easily find an eligible woman like Tina! She and her husband had to act now, if possible. It did not bother her at all that her son did not attend university or that he did not finish high school, and especially the fact that Tina was an outstanding political science graduate or that she was planning to do her graduate studies in a foreign country, and therefore may not be an appropriate match for her son. For her, educa-tion was a means to an end, and the end is marrying a good man and rais-ing a good family. Home, not a scientific laboratory, archaeological dig, a member of an executive board of a corporation, or a lecture hall in some of the fields of the humanities is the proper place for women. The preeminent concern of a young woman should be a secure life. Her family is her shelter.

"What is the purpose of Johannes's visit to Latakia?" Nora asked Ar-men when she was peeling a cucumber. "What is he doing here?" Frankly, Nora knew the purpose of Johannes's visit because her husband had com-municated to her not only information about Johannes but also his own opinion of his character.

"He is a historian, and is interested in the development of the political and cultural institutions of ancient Greek and Roman civilizations in Syria." Armen said and, turning her face toward Tina, asked, "Please, honey, can you and Jeannette prepare the araq and appetizers for the men?"

"Yes, mother. In addition to history, Johannes is interested in political science." Nora, who, like her husband, had not attended university, was afraid to reveal her ignorance of the nature of these two academic fields.

"He seems to be more interested in marriage than in research," Nora observed when Tina and Jeannette left the kitchen, one with a tray of araq and the second with a tray of appetizers. "He seems to have made a reputation for himself among the bachelor women of the church—"

"Impossible!" Deema intervened. "The young man has been spending his time secluded in his apartment writing or visiting historical sites. Studying the remains of ancient buildings and cities and then examining the artifacts found in them demands effort and time. This is an arduous task. By the way, he was very impressed by Ugarite. He thinks that the Phoenicians played a significant role in the development of ancient Greek civilization. Jirji told me that he has not met anybody in Bouqa or Latakia yet. He believes that Johannes is a committed scholar."

"Rumors fly fast and wide in this town," Armen remarked. "We should not hastily believe what we hear."

"I do not know anything about Johannes," Nora said sheepishly. I just said what I heard. His cousins, Nick and Nadim, like him very much. But Aunt Rachel is peeved at him—"

"Why?" Deema asked.

"Because he did not condole her immediately after her husband died. All the relatives and friends visited her but not Johannes. She could not understand why he did not visit her."

"I have a hunch," Deema remarked, "that he does not know our customs. Maybe Jirji should bring this matter to his attention. I am sure he is not trying to avoid anybody in the family. He does not even know them, at least not all of them! My impression is that he is pressed for time at this stage of his work."

"I tend to agree with Deema," Jeannette intervened, "he strikes me as a shy person. He does not know our ways. He needs a little time and a dash of encouragement."

"It would be a good idea if you tell the men that dinner will be ready in about fifteen minutes," Armen said. "Fill their araq glasses if they are empty and see if they need another round of appetizers."

A heated discussion was in progress when Tina and Jeannette entered the living room. "Please, both of you sit here. You will be needed in our debate, Tina," Nick said, interrupting Yuri's speech.

"Debate?" Tina exclaimed with a curious smile on her lips. "I am not a debater, and I doubt that I can make any meaningful contribution to any kind of debate, Uncle Nick."

"Me too!" Jeannette said, seconding Tina's response.

"But you should, Tina. You are a university graduate. If I am not mistaken, you distinguished yourself as an outstanding student in your department. You should be able to help Uncle Nadim." Tina and Jeannette did not know how to react to Nick's request. "I am confident that both of you will render a most needed assistance. Your father and Jirji are expert speakers. I am not."

"How can I, Jeannette, or anyone else help if we do not know the topic of the conversation and the position Uncle Nadim, or Uncle Jirji, or my father is defending? What if my view is contrary to Uncle Nadim's or yours?" Yuri smiled when he heard his daughter's response to Nick. "Anyway, what is the subject of the conversation?" Tina asked.

"Should university education be compulsory?"

"Compulsory?" Tina's asked with an expression of surprise in her face.

"Yes, compulsory, the way high school education is compulsory."

"For men and women, or only for men?" Jeannette's eyes glistened with suppressed tears when she heard the topic of the debate but remained silent. Has her Uncle forgotten that her father, Abraham, forbade her to attend university? Has he forgotten that he, like the rest of the Mitya men, except for Jirji, were chauvinists? She was so drowned in frustration, in self-pity, in anger, she could neither think nor speak. She looked at her Uncle sadly.

But in his way and for his reasons, Nick was also confused. He did not know how to answer Tina's question. "Nevertheless," Tina pressed on, "Uncle Jirji and my father should debate this question. I hope you proceed in your conversation with the assumption that university education should be compulsory for both women and men. My father is head of the education department in the Latakia district, and Uncle Jirji is a theologian, teaching the humanities at the College of the Holy Land. They are the right people for conducting this type of discussion."

"Still, you are a graduate student and plan to attend graduate school," Nick emphasized, "and you, Jeannette, should take part in this conversation."

"How can I take part in this conversation if women are not entitled to a university education just as men are?"

"Yes, compulsory education should include men and women," Nick said reluctantly. The tears that were suppressed in Jeannette's eyes earlier began to flow over her cheeks. Luckily, no one but Tina noticed them. She created an artificial cough and covered her face with a handkerchief she pulled out of her side pocket. Tina was the only person in that room who *could* notice those tears and feel the heart that gave birth to them. Jeanette graduated from high school with the highest grade in mathematics, and she was hailed by the ministry of education as one of the best students in many years and recommended that she should continue her studies in mathematics. Jeannette even received a scholarship to attend the University of Paris or any university of her choice, but her father forced her to decline it. "You should stay at home with your mother and grandmother," he told her. Jirji tried his best to change his cousin's mind, but, as everyone who knew him well, said, he was the most stubborn man in the family and maybe in the district of Latakia. "Uncle Abraham's head," his sister-in-law, Jameela, said, 'is really the head of a bull. If you open up his skull, you will find a huge flintstone there. You can argue with the devil, but not with Abraham!' Like his mother, he was convinced that the proper place of the woman was her home. Woman was ordained by God to be a homemaker: wife, mother, and house manager. The sinister aspect of this kind of chauvinism is that after a while, women feel and think that they are inferior to men and that their proper place is their home!

"Nick's response was followed by an unexpected endorsement from Jirji. "No one can forget that you were valedictorian in your graduating class. You are a very bright person. I am convinced that you can participate in a discussion on this and any other topic. Your capacity of comprehension, my dear, surpasses the capacity of most young people who graduate from Joul Jammal!" Jeannette did not comment on Jirji's endorsement but allowed a cynical smirk to hover over her lips.

"Why don't you and Tina join us?" Nick said as he pointed to two empty chairs. But the young women did not join the men. "We came only to see if you needed another round of araq and appetizers. Dinner will be served shortly."

"Yes, honey, you can bring us another round of araq," Yuri said. He looked at the plate of appetizers and added, "and a round of appetizers."

Tina and Jeannette left the room, and the conversation began. "I submit that university education is a necessary condition of human happiness. Every citizen, man, and woman should be obliged to go to university," Jirji said. The mere statement of this proposition made Nick cringe.

"We can hardly enforce the existing law that high school education should be mandatory. Illiteracy is more prevalent than you think. Ask Yuri. He is an expert on state education in the country. But first, how can you justify your proposal? Second, suppose it is justifiable, and I strongly doubt that it is, how can you convince the Parliament, which is a bunch of chauvinists, to legislate a law of mandatory university education?"

"I shall be happy to respond to your first question, but I think Yuri should answer the second question." Yuri smiled without uttering a word.

"Let us hear your justification," Nick said defiantly.

"Every human being is entitled to happiness. Happiness is a fundamental human right. Attainment of this right is the supreme aspiration of all human beings. Everything people do points to this aspiration. If you ask any person why they act in a certain way, their answer would, directly or indirectly, involve their level of happiness. It stands to reason that no one desires to harm themselves or do anything that may harm them now or in the future. Moreover, ask yourself, Nick, why do people, as individuals and as societies, do their best to promote science, art, philosophy, education, and technology? Why do they build those magnificent systems of government, those cultural, artistic, scientific, technological, religious, economic, legal, and social institutions, and organizations? Might it be that the wellbeing, the happiness, of the people is the sole reason for all these types of activities and pursuits? Put differently, these institutions exist to an end, and the end is human happiness. They are frameworks within which individuals can achieve their happiness. Now, let me state that university education is a necessary condition for happiness."

"Why?" Nadim asked.

"One moment, please!" Yuri interjected. "Our drinks have arrived. Tina and Jeannette placed the drinks and appetizers on the make-shift tables. "It would be a good idea if you join us," Yuri addressed the young ladies.

"We are needed in the kitchen, Father," Tina responded, "but we shall be back as soon as possible."

"But why is university education a necessary condition of happiness?" Nadim asked again.

"Because these conditions create a context for the citizens not only to pursue the kind of life-projects whose realization makes them happy but also to cultivate the art of making sound judgments. A person who cannot make a sound judgment during the administration of their life is bound to be unhappy. Consequently, since education is a human right, and it is since the state is obligated to secure the conditions for the attainment of this right, university education should be mandatory. In the past, high school education was enough because life was simple, but now it is becoming increasingly technologized, increasingly complex, and increasingly demanding intellectually, socially, culturally, economically, morally, and politically! Here, I assume that education is a means to end. The end is human enlightenment, and human enlightenment is a necessary condition for making sound judgment, and sound judgment is, in turn, an essential requirement of happiness.

"Students do not any more acquire an in-depth understanding of the basic concepts, theories, and principles of contemporary science, philosophy, religion, art, and technology. They are not allowed to cultivate their logical, analytical, evaluative, and communicative skills, and they do not learn how to utilize the knowledge they receive in understanding themselves and the meaning of human life and destiny or even how to develop and nourish a vocation. They receive snippets of knowledge in some of the basic areas of science, art, technology, and philosophy but not a comprehensive view of the map of this knowledge. But that is not enough. We should always remember that little knowledge can be dangerous: How can such snippets help rising students find their way in their practical lives, much less succeed in designing their life-projects? Again, at this level of education, the emphasis is mostly on memorizing ideas, generalizations, and certain principles and rules, not on the development of the powers of the mind—"

"Where do you live, Jirji," Nadim asked, interrupting his cousin, "on earth or in the kingdom of heaven?" This reaction from Nadim elicited a chuckle from Nick and a stare from Yuri. Although the chuckle did not last long, the stare did, because Nadim's wife, Sarah, suddenly appeared at the door of the living room and fastened her eyes on her husband. No one knew what transpired in the silent dialogue between those eyes, but the cousins knew its outcome because Nadim immediately stood up and asked Nick to supplant him. On his way out of the room, he said, "Please continue the conversation. I shall be back shortly." Yuri looked curiously at his guests and, without uttering a word, sped after Nadim.

Left alone, the cousins exchanged silent but restless stares for a few seconds. A wind of suspense swept through the space that separated them from each other. Their desire to know the cause of Nadim's abrupt departure was intense. But their curiosity was pacified, at least temporarily, when Yuri returned to the living room with "Let us continue the conversation." But Nick was not mollified. Except for Johannes, who was still ignorant regarding the psyche and ethos of the Mitya family in Latakia, the cousins were convinced that something grave, maybe dire, compelled Nadim and his wife to leave that important dinner. Their fear was confirmed by Yuri's grave concern.

"There must be something wrong!" Nick remarked. "Today is Sunday. As far as I know, Nadim and his wife always stay at home on Sundays."

"No one of the ladies in the kitchen was informed of the reason that prompted Nadim and his wife to leave in such an abrupt manner," Yuri added, "but we shall soon find out. Tina is on her way to their house now. In the meantime, it would be wise to continue our most interesting conversation. I am profoundly interested in it, and I plan to express my opinion on the question of compulsory university education a bit later."

Although reluctantly, for he had a presentiment that a critical problem compelled Nadim and his wife to leave the Sarkisians just before dinner time, Nick said to Jirji, "your conception of enlightenment as a condition of happiness is highly romantic, highly unrealistic. It can never be implemented in the near or distant future."

"It may seem romantic, but it is certainly idealistic and therefore feasible in the foreseeable or distant future, if not now. The concept of an enlightened individual, I propose, should be viewed as an ideal we can justifiably strive for. We can also use it as a standard in evaluating the weaknesses and strengths of the existing programs of education, but more importantly, we can treat it as a guideline in our endeavor to construct an educational program or reform an existing one. Any program that is not designed or reformed according to an ideal—a standard, vision, or rational purpose—is bound to fail. For example, the recent advances in science, technology, art, and economics rendered the established curricula of the many universities of the world somewhat out of date. The question we now face is how to update them? Can we update them without a vision, a conception of a reasonable idea of education, one that utilizes the most recent advances in the different areas of human knowledge and values? The concept of an enlightened person, I suggested, can, I think, function as a basis in updating the curricula of the different institutions of higher learning. In this case, we do not only incorporate the recent advances in science, art, technology, and economics, we also incorporate them with an eye on the enlightenment of the youth as the aim of education. It is not enough to know these advances; it is crucially important to understand the significance and role of these areas of knowledge in human life."

Nick did not comment on Jirji's response to his objection. He retrieved his araq glass from the tray sitting next to him and almost emptied the glass in one gulp. He stared at Yuri with troubled eyes and then said to Jirji, "You had the privilege of attending university; I did not. I doubt that I can converse with you competently on the nature and aim of education. The person who should comment on your proposal is Yuri. He is one of the most knowledgeable people in the area of education in the city of Latakia. Even the ministry of education frequently asks for his advice on the design or implementation of certain programs." Nick paused, looked at Yuri, and continued, "You cannot deny this Yuri. This man has been unusually quiet today. I do not know why, but if he has a good reason to refrain from participating in this conversation, I recommend that Johannes be my replacement. Everyone says that he is a highly educated man."

"But I am not an expert in education. I am a student of history and political science."

"Still, you are more qualified than I to discuss the aims of education."

"I second Nick's recommendation." Yuri intervened.

"You have no choice, Johannes. But before you take over, I have a strong desire to direct a question to Jirji?"

"What is it?" Jirji asked.

"What does education have to do with happiness? I do not see any type of relationship between them. The majority of people in the world, now and in the past, did not go to school—do you mean to say that they are not happy or that they cannot be happy? As far as I know, we learn how to be happy from our parents, elders, peers, teachers, religious institutions, and especially from personal experience in the different spheres of our lives. And, let me tell you, Jirji, that most of the people who go to high school, even to university, put aside their education and learn what life is about, and especially what makes them happy after they become active members of society. They study science, history, mathematics, literature, philosophy, and social studies, and sometimes they learn how to draw pictures or how to sing, but they do not learn how to be happy. Not one of the teachers in any of these and other academic fields teach the student how to lead a happy life. The source of happiness is living according to the life-projects we choose during our daily lives, not the abstract ideas we learn in school. These ideas may be interesting, useful in some ways, and I would say an intellectual luxury, but they are not that essential to the attainment of happiness. This attainment is an individual responsibility from beginning to end. It originates from self-understanding and the extent to which the individual succeeds in realizing it. My grandfather used to say that the more we know about the world and its questions and problems, the more miserable we become. Our life is a field, and we should be the peasants of this field. My grandfather may be wrong, and if he is, he cannot be completely wrong."

"What do you mean by 'happiness'—?" Jirji asked.

This exchange was interrupted by Jeannette's appearance. "Dinner is served!" She announced with a sad voice and an even sadder expression. Yuri stood up and extended a cordial invitation to his guests to move to the dining room, which was practically an extension of the living room. "We can continue this conversation at the dinner table. You can bring your drinks with you," he added.

Three women dressed in black were seated at the dining table. The assortment of dishes laid out on the table was amazingly impressive. One large bottle of beer sat on each one of its ends and a bottle of wine in its middle. A stranger would say that it was fit for a regal occasion. Yuri sat at one end and Armen at the other. Jirji sat on Armen's right side and his wife at Yuri's right hand. Johannes sat next to Jirji. Tina's chair was vacant. The first thing Yuri did when he sat down was to welcome his guests, but his welcome was painfully subdued primarily because he had a strong feeling that a violent storm was brewing in the sky of the Mitya family. Armen, who knew her husband quite well, felt the sad tone of his welcome, which was general and lacking in the warmth she was expecting. So, to remedy this situation, she said the following: "We are delighted to welcome the newly discovered member of the Mitya family. We wish you a successful adventure in Latakia, Johannes. Please, view the Sarkisian family as an extension of the Mitya family. You are at home today!"

"I second Armen's welcome!" Jirji said as he raised his araq glass to his lips. Yuri followed suit but not Nick. Although he was genial and very courteous to his German cousin, he did not trust him, not only because Uncle Mikhail's story that his cousin Hanania was a bastard was dubious but also because he felt that Johannes was about to "snatch" Tina from him as his future daughter-in-law. But Armen's cheerful welcome did not last long because it was followed by a chilling lull: an expectation of bad news dominated their minds, but not Johannes's, most likely because he was still ignorant of the members and lives of the Mitya family. Soon after he sampled the main dishes that attracted his culinary interest, he said, "I would like to thank the ladies who prepared these delectable dishes. They are truly luscious! He filled an empty glass placed next to his plate with wine and added, "I felt fortunate when I met my cousins and most of my family in Latakia, but now I feel honored to meet their friends and share equally beautiful moments with them!" This compliment summoned a smile on Armen's lips, which she suppressed, and a response from Yuri, in which he declared: "The Mitya family are dear to our hearts. From now on, our home is your home, Johannes!"

Neither Johannes's expression of appreciation nor Yuri's welcome dispelled the chilling lull that seemed to grow thicker with every passing moment. However, it was dismissed a few seconds later by the sound of the front door opening and then closing. The suspense was mounting in the minds of the Mitya family members and Tina's entrance into the dining room. All eyes were directed at her. She sat in her chair but could not speak. Her face was a glittering image of melancholy of gloom. She poured some beer in her glass, took a sip from it, and with a tight knot on her brow, said, "I am sorry to be the bearer of bad tidings."

"We are adults, honey," her father intervened, "go ahead!"

"Bassam, Uncle Nadim's son, is now in jail and will soon be moved to a maximum-security cell in the Latakia penitentiary." 'Os' and 'whats' resounded throughout the room, and wide eyes fired expressions of shock and disbelief toward the bearer of the bad tidings! Tina felt them, and she felt guilty for being the messenger of distressing news.

"Why?" Nick cried with a trembling voice. His shoulders were twitching, and his eyes were as wild as the eyes of a raging bull. "Why?" he repeated, "Speak, Tina!" Nick was devastated.

"He and one of his friends," Tina continued, "were apprehended by the police in the middle of a very violent brawl with two men. Bassam and his friend beat one of them to death. When they inspected his car, the police discovered two kilos of cocaine under the driver's seat and a very large bundle of U.S. dollars. The city is abuzz with the news of this crime."

"Do you mean that my nephew is a killer and a drug dealer? Impossible!"

"I do not mean anything, Uncle Nick, I am only reporting what Aunt Sarah told me," Tina said timidly. "The police know that he is a black marketeer," Tina continued, "but this time they caught him in a fight and a murder. No one knows the cause of the brawl, but one policeman who was involved in the investigation of his case and knows Uncle Nadim said that Bassam and his friend were under the influence of more than one kind of drug. It is a very messy situation," Tina said, and turning her face toward Jriji added, "Uncle Nadim needs you. He is inconsolable. He and Aunt Sarah are so confused, so embarrassed, so devastated, they do not know what to say or do."

With sorrow in his eyes and a heavy heart, Jirji stood, moved toward his wife, and kissed her, then he embraced his hostess and thanked Yuri. "Wait, Jirji," Nick said, "I shall come with you! He, too, thanked Armen and Yuri before leaving the dining room. Yuri accompanied them to the front door. "Let me know what happens. Don't hesitate to call me if you need any help!" he said.

"I shall!"

Silence reigned despotically when Jirji and Nick left the Sarkisian house. It was a cathartic moment of silence. Regardless of whether it is cheerful or painful, the recession of a strong feeling of suspense, one precipitated by a tense, dramatic course of events or one that surprises us with dire or disastrous expectations, tends to produce a sense of inner calm, a kind of psychological lull. Jeannette, who knew the inner workings of the family, its ethos, its strengths, weaknesses, secrets, and scandals, shattered that cathartic silence. "Jirji is the spiritual father of the family. He can do many things no one of his cousins can do, but I doubt that he can create miracles. I sometimes think that there are about two rotten fruits in every box of tomatoes. It seems hard, and I think impossible, to restore a rotten tomato to its original state of health. Bassam is one of the rotten tomatoes in the Mitya family. We shall sooner or later discover who the other rotten fruit is." A cynical smirk crept over Yuri's lips. He felt a strong desire to comment on Jeannette's insipid comment about Jirji and why some children go astray and fall in a puddle of social muck, but he did not. He knew that, regardless of whether she knew it, she raised one of the most challenging questions philosophers and social scientists have been struggling with for centuries; he also knew that she should have been a participant in the conversation on the aims of education a little while ago. Jeannette's remark provoked a storm of ideas and recalcitrant questions in his mind, but for some reason, he chose to remain silent. He threw a look at his wife, who, too, was looking at him and nodded.

"Why don't we clear the table and continue our visit in the living room?" Armen suggested.

"This is a good idea!" Tina returned.

"Before leaving this room," Johannes said, "let me express my profound gratitude and appreciation for this most delicious meal," he frowned a little and added, "the news of Bassam's crime and his arrest are debilitating. I cannot help but feel the hurt and anguish of Uncle Nadim and his wife and the whole family for the misery that befell them. I shall commiserate with them as soon as possible. But despite this sad turn of events, I must recognize the warmth, generosity, and human excellence I felt in this house today. I am honored to be the recipient of this privilege, and I should say a gift. I shall always cherish it." He turned his attention first toward Armen and then toward Yuri and continued, "The hands that create goodness in so many ways are touched by the hands of the divine." Johannes was blushing when he made this impromptu speech. He was so flustered, he almost quivered. Impulsively, he picked up his plate with one hand and his empty glass with the other to take them to the kitchen. Armen stretched her arm and held his arm. "You are in Latakia, my dear!" She said. "Why don't you, Jeannette, Yuri, and Tina go to the living room? Deema and I will join you shortly."

"It is good to help," Johannes remarked, "and it is better to share."

"It is good, and I think it is lovely," Armen replied, "but not today." Johannes bit his lower lip softly and left the table with Yuri and the two young ladies.

"Is he a Mitya?" Armen asked when she and Deema were cleaning the plates and putting them up.

"Yes, Jirji told me that he is a genuine Mitya."

"I did not mean biologically. I meant—"

"Oh, no, he is not!" Deema interrupted Armen. "Jirji mentioned that he is closer to Johannes than to any of his Latakia cousins."

"I felt sorry for him when he tried to thank Yuri and me. He is a very thoughtful and sensitive person. I have a feeling that he grew up among books, not among real human beings. People like him are frequently manipulated and abused, especially in a business-minded society like ours. I think Jirji should keep a careful eye on him."

"I agree with you. He strikes me as a highly learned individual, but also as an innocent and naïve man. Jirji mentioned that the research he is doing in Syria will be the basis of a two-volume book. He hopes that the book will qualify him for a full professorship."

"I wish him good luck!"

"I do too!"

"There you are!" Yuri said when Armen and Deema entered the living room. "Johannes and Tina are in the middle of a conversation on one of the underlying conditions of democracy as a form of government."

"What conditions?" Armen asked.

"If the people are the source of political authority, the question we should ask is *who these people are.* Here, it is assumed that a society is free since it is the source of the authority that governs them. In the ancient Athenian *polis,* the cradle of Western democracy, most of the people were ethnically, religiously, historically, and culturally homogeneous; moreover, the polis was small. So, *all the people* were able to elect their leaders, but now 'all the people' cannot participate in this kind of process because most, if not all, the societies of the world are vast, heterogeneous, culturally, ethnically, religiously, economically, and ideologically. The critical question," Tina insisted, "is this: Is the election of the legislators and the leaders, in general, the defining feature of democracy? If, in a given democracy, direct representation is not possible, how can it be a democracy? And if it is not a democracy, can we say it is a free society? Is it possible to have a free society without the election of the leaders by the people? What is the defining feature of democracy—freedom or direct election of leaders by the people? Is the election of representatives the only process that leads to a free society? What is the essential nature of democracy?"

"That is a unique way of articulating the main question of democracy," Johannes remarked. Both Armen and Yuri looked reflectively at their daughter. She was not the young woman she used to be any longer. She was already an adult—a woman! She was conversing with Johannes not as a student but as a thinker, as a mind that analyzes concepts and problems logically, critically. She was a woman who stood on her own feet. It suddenly occurred to her parents that they, too, were growing with her. How could they be the same parents if their daughter was a woman?

A flood of emotions crowded Armen's mind. She was unable to focus her attention on the essential nature of democracy. She felt like she abruptly received the highest reward she had been expecting all her adult life! She was captive to a unique, unprecedented kind of thrill. A smile forced itself on her lips. "Please, my dear," she said addressing Tina, "why don't you continue your conversation with Johannes. Deema and I would be happy to listen to you!"

"I shall give you a precis of the ideas they had discussed earlier," Yuri said.

"Great!"

"Several political thinkers tend to emphasize the etymology of 'democracy'—*demos and kratos*; they argue that democracy is a society in which the people govern, or one in which the people are the source of political power. This implies a rejection of monarchy, despotism, or any form of autocracy. The supreme value that underlies this type of government is freedom: a free society is a self-governed society. This is the view you espouse, Johannes—am I correct?" Tina asked.

"Yes, to a large extent," Johannes replied.

"But this view is an oblique reiteration of the ancient Athenian conception of democracy. I reject it."

"Why?"

"Because, as I have just pointed out, the conception of Athenian democracy does not apply to today's liberal and pluralistic society. The interests of the people are as diverse as they are religious, cultural, aesthetic, economic, ethnic, and ideological. It is impossible to elect their representatives directly. This is why the masters of political philosophy in the seventeenth and eighteenth centuries suggested the idea of electing a government that represents their interests. Allow me to highlight this point, Johannes."

"Please, do!"

"The elected leaders cannot represent the people. Representing them is tantamount to relinquishing their wills to the government they elect, but the human will cannot be relinquished or transferred to any agency, for this entails relinquishing their freedom, which is impossible because the very purpose of democracy is the attainment of freedom. The foundation of a democratic political system is law, not the will of any individual or group of individuals. Law is the authority that governs, and in a democracy, the law expresses or represents the interests of the people. One of the basic tasks of government is the articulation of these interests into law. This is why, as the principle of justice, the law is valid since it expresses, or serves, the interests of the people."

"But," Johannes interjected, "as you have just indicated, contemporary society is large and diverse in its interests—how can it embody the interests of all the people equally?"

"It cannot. This is why many scholars think, as you know, that, since the interests of all the people cannot be served equally, the interests of the majority is the second-best option. And in fact, the governments of the living democracies of the contemporary world are founded in the will of the majority, assuming that the majority is enlightened and rational. But how can such a government be truly just? Is the government that does not represent the interests of all its people equally truly democratic, especially when the minority is sometimes about forty to forty-eight percent of the population?

"Besides, the mere erection of a democratic system of government is not enough. For some strange reason, it suffers from an inherent weakness. Not all elected officials are competent and trustworthy. Political corruption has always been the cancer of the different types of government in the world. This is a big question that needs a separate conversation, but now let me remark that contemporary democracy seems to be susceptible to this kind of cancer. Once a bureaucracy is established, it seems hard to change it! In principle, it can be reformed, but this task is mostly impossible!"

"Is this cancer inherent in democracy or in human nature?"

"In human nature, this is the main reason why it is inherent in democracy."

"Some democracies have introduced a system of checks and balances to prevent, or at least minimize, corruption," Johannes pointed out.

"Yes, most of the time, this system does not work, at least not effectively. Sooner or later, it becomes incorporated in the bureaucracy, which frequently happens in large states. The capitalists that are lustful for power and money do not only *buy* the representatives but also the committees that are supposed to oversee their activities, of course not exactly like the commodities we buy in the market-place but through an amazingly complex network of legally approved influence. They proceed on the assumption that everyone in this world has a price, not on the assumption that politicians are political angels. When you control the legislative and executive branches of government, you can pass the policies you desire. It is strange, very strange, indeed, when these laws serve the interests of the few without sufficient or fair respect for the interests of the minority. We should always remember that the minority are human beings, that they are citizens, and that they are entitled to equal treatment by the government.

"Presently, almost every basic institution, even education, and the law are to a large extent being 'politicized.' I think that economic power tends to over-ride political power in the majority of the world states. I believe that it does not matter what kind of power rules a country as long as it is just, but, unfortunately, as experience teaches, the impulse of greed in human nature is powerful. This is why we should be wary when societies are governed by people who are receptive to this impulse."

"I agree with you about the increasing dominance of economic power and corruption, and so of the capitalists, in most of the countries of the world, but let me ask a question that your remark about corruption has stirred in my mind: Do you think that all political officials are corrupt or corruptible?"

"There are good human beings in the world, therefore, there must be decent, incorruptible political officials. You may accuse me of cynicism if I tell you that the good people you seem to have in mind are withdrawing from, if not shunning, the sphere of politics primarily because they know that they cannot function as honest politicians. Sadly, most of the politicians we see on the stage of national and international politics are cunning, loquacious, discreet, effective dealers, but not truly *just* political officials! And if they are just, it is only to a minimal extent. Greedy capitalists thrive on corruption. Moreover, competent political officials are impotent in the face of the realistic— and shall we say, Machiavellian?—impotent political officials and widespread corruption. Can they, or should, they sacrifice their lives at the altar of corruption? As you know, even in the advanced countries of the Western world, whether in legislatures, schools, corporations, decision-making committees in the main sectors of public life, the people who make laws and policies are the majority. And the minority?

"I am not unaware of the fact that many of the Western, and some of the non-democracies of the world, have admirably promoted education, science, art, philosophy, technology, and the material well-being their people, and I hope this trend continues. We should always remember that any form of government, regardless of whether it is democratic, monarchical, or autocratic, is a means to an end, and the end is or should be, the freedom of the citizens. This freedom is what justifies the legitimacy of a specific government.

"But the point that merits special emphasis is that the real power that governs the different societies of the world is not 'the people.' The capitalists may promote the well-being of the masses, but they do so only in so far as this is a factor in the promotion of their own-wellbeing, not out of love, or respect for the humanity of the poor, the sick, the disenfranchised, or the ignorant. On the contrary, their basic principle is that what is good for the capitalists is good for society. They reverse the fundamental argument of the major political philosophers and the collective wisdom of enlightened minds ever since human civilization saw the light of day! But, if societies do no rule themselves, even if they have a democratic system of government, can we call these systems real democracies? I do not wish to open up the Pandora 's Box of political theory and practice, of which you are more cognizant than I, but I am compelled to say that real democracy remains a farfetched ideal. What calls for special notice here is that the so-called great democracies of the world are governed more by greedy capitalists than by wise leaders. They do their best either to seduce or to directly pressure the less developed countries to adopt their system of government, of course, in the name of freedom, human rights, prosperity, peace, and progress. But can democracy or any form of government be imported, exported, or imposed on another society? If a good government is founded in law, if the law originates from the will of the people or expresses their interests, how can we impose any form of government on another society? A type of government is not a commodity we can buy or sell; it should reflect a way of life, one that originates from the bosom of its culture. Even in Northern Europe, where you live, Johannes, no two democracies are alike, even though they are alike in electing their political leaders and upholding human rights. Didn't the idea of democracy originate from the bosom of Western culture? Why shouldn't every society choose its form of government? Freedom, not merely election, is the defining feature of the just or functional state.

"Now, does it matter what form of government a state chooses as long as freedom and justice guides its laws and policies, that is, as long as its institutions provide the conditions of human freedom? Can it provide such conditions if the laws that govern its practical life do not embody or express the interests of all its people? Shouldn't such a state create a mechanism that synthesizes, or reconciles, the interests of the different interests of its pluralistic society?" Johannes's eyes, which were focused on Tina's lips, as she spoke, remained tethered to them after she stopped talking! Armen and Yuri, who were stunned by the erudition, logic, moral heart, and understanding of their daughter, were drunk with an exhilarating feeling of pride. They were deeply impressed by her critique of contemporary democracy. But Tina was oblivious to Johannes's eyes and her parents' sense of pride or amazement. She stopped for a moment and with a serious frown on her forehead continued, "I am afraid that the capitalists of the Western world have packaged the ideal of democracy in the most attractive colors and placed it in the market of international politics not because they are interested in promoting democracy or the wellbeing of the developing world but as a means to colonizing them economically, technologically, culturally, and educationally. Let me hasten to add that I am not opposed to capitalism. I am opposed to exploitation, oppression, greed, injustice, and selfishness. Contemporary capitalism is a hotbed for these evils. Any society that neglects its intellectual, moral, and spiritual advancement is bound to fail."

"Would you say, then," Johannes intervened," that valid law, not necessarily this or that form of government, should be the instrument by which a people should be governed?"

Tina could not respond to Johannes's question because Jeannette, who has been waiting for the right moment to interrupt the conversation, signaled, by raising her hand, that time was up: "I am sorry to break off this valuable conversation." She looked apologetically at Yuri and Armen and then at Johannes. "We need to leave. Aunt Rachel must be waiting for us. She is anxious to see Johannes."

"We understand," Yuri said. "You and Tina should continue this conversation at another time, hopefully soon. It is unfair to whet our appetite about this exciting topic without allowing us to know the conditions under which valid law can be implemented effectively."

"I gladly accept your proposal. But I confess that I cannot make any constructive contribution to this subject without Tina's help. In fact, she was the actual author of this conversation today."

"I am only a student!" Tina emphasized vehemently. A blush surged on her cheeks.

"Neither truth nor wisdom is earned by age or academic rank," Johannes said with a tender voice. "But allow me to say that you should continue your studies in the area of political philosophy. You are not a student;

you are an inquirer. The world is in urgent need of inquirers—of seekers of knowledge in all its forms."

"You give me more credit than I deserve."

"If I give you more credit than you deserve, I inflict harm on you, but I would never do this to you or to anybody else." Johannes said, and then looking at Yuri, and Armen added, "please, accept my gratitude for a wonderful day." He moved toward Armen and hugged her, and then shook hands with Yuri. Jeannette led Johannes to Aunt Rachel's house.

SIX

Tina and Johannes Fall in Love

A LOUD WHIR WAS bursting out of the doors and windows of the Mitya building when Jeannette and Johannes ascended the stairs that led to Abraham and Hanania's house. "It is Sunday!" Jeannette remarked. "Most of the children come at this time to see their great grandmother. They always kissed her hand and left with an allowance in theirs. Some of the children looked forward to greeting the Matriarch not so much because they liked or disliked her but because they expected an allowance and a piece of chocolate or bonbon from her. On days such as Easter or Christmas, she gave them one or two pieces of marzipan or honey pastries. Even though she was diabetic, she always had a box of sweets under her divan. In this family, offering someone a sweet is a gesture of fondness, approval, or esteem. "But there were no allowances or sweets during the mourning month, and there were no children in her room when Jeannette and Johannes came to visit her that afternoon. They were playing on the patio. Contrary to her long-established practice, Aunt Rachel remained seated on the right side of the divan. This was her way of expressing her disapproval of Johannes's behavior toward her. He bent his tall body and kissed her three times on the cheeks. She did not return his kisses, but she acknowledged his greeting and asked him to sit in a chair close to the divan. It was clear to Jeannette, who sat next to her, that she was vexed with the German Mitya. She wanted to come to Johannes's defense, for she knew that he was in for a sharp reprimand, but she could not, because Aunt Rachel promptly said:

"How is it that you have not come to see me until now? You knew Mikhail died several days ago, you even attended his funeral, and you visited with several members of the family, but not me—why? Respect for the elders is a must in this family!" What a reprimand! Jeannette cringed, and Johannes flinched. He did not know how to react to this harsh and unjustifiable rebuke. He looked at his cousin seeking help, but she was flabbergasted, helpless! "I have been eager to hear news about our family in Germany," Aunt Rachel added, "but you have acted like I do not exist. This is not the Mitya way!"

Jeannette, who could no longer bear the injustice of this harsh and inexcusable rebuke, interrupted her grandmother. "Johannes has been very busy. He has not visited anybody in the family yet. His time is limited. Besides, he does not know our customs. You are the first person he visits."

"Aunt Rachel," Johannes said with a conciliatory tone in his voice, "I am very sorry for delaying my visit until now," and with a cheerful face and smiling lips, he added, "you are as beautiful as my grandfather said. I am so happy I was finally able to meet you." Aunt Rachel suppressed a smile when she heard those complimentary words, and continued her rebuke but in a rather cheerful spirit.

"You should stay here with us. The ground floor, where Mikhail used to live, is now empty."

"But I am—" Johannes tried to explain why he could not move to the Mitya building but to no avail.

"You don't have to worry about moving your things. Uncle Abraham will take care of that chore."

"Johannes needs to be in Bouqa," Jeannette intervened, "his kind of work requires him to be there."

With Jeannette's help and Johannes's kind heart, Aunt Rachel was reconciled with the son of her brother-in-law and listened intently to the wealth of information he conveyed to her about the German branch of the family. She even kissed him on the cheek when he left her and proceeded with Jeannette to the living room.

Nick and Hanania were engaged in what seemed to Jeannette an earnest conversation, to the extent that they were conducting it in whispering voices. Nick was practically talking with his body. His arms were flying through the air in all directions, his head was shaking vehemently, and his eyes were shooting sparks of anger. Hanania was listening to him, looking confused. Both men stopped talking when the German and his cousin entered the room. Johannes sped toward Hanania, kissed him on the cheeks three times, and said, "I am truly sorry for your loss, Uncle!"

"This is God's will, not ours, son," Hanania said and asked Jeannette to sit next to him.

"What is the latest news, Uncle?" she asked. My grandmother said that it is worse than expected.

"Yes, it is. Your cousin, Faris, will also be in jail sometime later this evening—"

"Why?" Johannes exclaimed. He was shaken, so was Jeannette. "Who is Faris?"

"He is Uncle Abraham's middle son."

"Why is he sought by the police?

"He was involved in the brawl with his cousin, Bassam, but indirectly."

"How?"

"The situation is complicated," Nick said. Faris is well known as a money black marketeer. Everyone in the business community is aware of this fact mainly because they deal with him. He has been on the watch list of the secret service because he was apprehended by them several times over the past few years. He was always able to receive a pardon by bribing the right officials. Apparently, Bassam's friend, who was involved in the fight, betrayed him. In an attempt to negate the severity of his crime, he told the police that the bundle of dollars they found in the car was provided by Faris as a part of a drug deal they were about to transact with another group of drug dealers. You see, Johannes, Uncle Abraham, is devastated and does not know what to do. He, Nadim, and Jirji are now in the bedroom trying to find a way to bail them out, at least Faris, since he is not accused of a capital crime. Faris's name is always on the list of possible suspects. Faris is a kind of mobile exchange bureau. His pockets are always filled with dollars and euros. They say he is the slickest money black marketeer in town. But this time he is in serious trouble!" Nick shook his head and continued: "No one can bail Bassam out. As for Faris, I doubt that he can be released from prison soon because he is charged with two violations, drug-dealing, and money black marketeering. You do not know the way the bureaucracy works in Latakia. Even if you can bribe everyone, it will take ages to get Faris released. Bassam's case is impossible. No one in that bureaucracy would accept your bribe—"

"Why?" Johannes interrupted.

"Fear."

"What do you mean?"

"Not of their superiors because all the superiors accept bribes, but of the family of the young man Bassam killed. They would readily kill Bassam, Faris, or any member of their families out of revenge. It is a complicated situation. One should be extra careful."

At that moment of the conversation, Nick's demeanor suddenly changed. A sardonic grin settled in the corners of his mouth. His shoulders twitched a little. He threw a wild, piercing, scrutinizing look at Johannes's face and instantly moved his eyes like a pendulum between Johannes's face and Hanania's. Neither Jeannette nor Hanania understood the meaning of that look; they thought that he was still reflecting on the obstacles that stood in the way of Faris's release, hopefully soon.

A bad, painful, disturbing, or harmful experience, one that leaves a wound on the wall of your mind can, by association, summon forth hidden, forgotten, or suppressed bad thoughts, desires, feelings, or encounters. This type of experience happens because the bad thoughts, feelings, or experiences are joined together causally by some law of association, so that if one of them is evoked the other or some of them tend to emerge as well. The basis of this association is the similarity of a certain quality or factor and is sometimes the mere contiguity of these experiences. In the present situation the presence of Johannes aroused the memory of a host of bad experiences: the recent elopement of his daughter, Mikhail's revelation that Aunt Rachel was an adulterer and that her son Hanania was a bastard, the possibility that Mikhail had revealed other dark secrets not only about his wife and sons but also about the rest of the family, the speculation that Johannes was a highly attractive bachelor and that he was about to "snatch" his future daughter-in-law from him—yes, these memories thronged his mind when his eyes moved like a pendulum between Hanania and Johannes.

When a barrage of bad memories surge into your consciousness, when their weight overwhelms its thinking capacity, your immediate response is to dispel them by some magical wand, to fight them with all your might until you crush them, to tease them away, if possible, to deny them, or to find an explanation that silences them. Nick did not like what he saw and what he felt when he scrutinized Hanania's and Johannes's faces. Hanania might, after all, be a bastard! Nick was miserable, and he wanted to get rid of the turmoil that was raging in his mind. The possibility that Johannes was the jinx of the Mitya family abruptly gripped his mind with an iron fist. "How can anyone explain this phenomenal sequence of events? Nothing but a jinx and a foreign jinx at that is suddenly in our midst! He must be the devil in the shape of a researcher! Why did all these calamities happen so soon and almost simultaneous with his arrival? I wish I could wipe him off the face of the earth!" He thought, and then he stared at Johannes one more time, his expression conveying sparks of his doubts, fears, and hatred. Nick did not care whether or how he would get rid of his German cousin or whether he was justified in blaming him for those calamities. He simply saw him as the source of the evils that were visiting his dear family and wished to destroy their source. He felt that the ground under his feet was unstable, shifty and that he was shifting with it. The faces he was comparing a second ago lost their identity. They were suddenly transformed into abstract images into jumbled configurations of eyes, ears, noses, cheeks, and foreheads loosely joined by an invisible thread. In a psychological state like this, one can act irrationally, violently, and rashly at any moment, and Nick was about to assault his German cousin.

It is strange how beauty and order recede from our eyes, and evil thoughts, feelings, emotions, weird visions, and desires advance into our minds. Nick's heart began to beat fast, and his eyes pierced one more defiant, vengeful, and hateful look at Johannes. A cynical grin flitted on his lips. His hand formed a fist. It was so hard, the nails of his fingers almost dug a hole into his palm. He felt an irresistible desire to level a fatal blow, one from which his cousin could not recover, and he was ready to repeat his blow again and again until he was absolutely sure that his victim was absolutely dead. He scrutinized his cousin's face with a sweet feeling of vengeance. But he could not move his fist from his lap because at that very moment Johannes, who discerned, by the power of empathy, that Nick was suffering from an intense flare of agony over the imprisonment of his nephews, not to mention the elopement of his daughter with a Durzi, embraced him with a compassionate gaze. This embrace was followed by a warm smile. It was clear to Jeannette that the love that emanated from Johannes's face relayed an intimate message: "You are not alone, Nick! We are with you, and will always be with you. We love you. Please, remember: These adversities will pass. Together, we can make them pass honorably." Neither Jeannette nor Hanania missed the message of that silent speech. It was inconceivable that Nick did not hear it! The radiance of that love lingered in Johannes's eyes and on Nick's face. It was difficult for Nick to resist the overwhelming effect of that emanation, but it was equally difficult to resist the voice of doubt that was gnawing at Nick's mind, not because he was a doubting Thomas but because he could not yet grasp the enormity of the calamities that seemed to be wrecking the foundation of his and his cousins' lives. The question "Why? Why us?" mockingly confronted him like a wild beast!

Jeannette, who felt the love that emanated from Johannes toward Nick in the fullness of its power, made a serious attempt to further assist her Uncle. She placed her right hand on his shoulder and was about to intervene, but her intervention was impeded by the sound of advancing steps. Jirji, Abraham, and Nadim walked into the living room. Ibrahim, Abraham's oldest son, who must have left them at the door, was heard saying, "I shall see you later, Dad."

The three cousins wore three equally grim expressions as they moved to their chairs. Jirji sat next to Johannes, Abraham next to Jeannette, and Nadim next to Nick. "I have never thought," Nick said after the five cousins exchanged apprehensive looks, "that the foundation of our family is crumbling. The house of the Mitya family has been sitting on sand, not on a solid rock. What is wrong with the new generation?"

"Every new generation is old to the preceding generation. Every generation is old and new at the same time, depending on how you look at it. The parents of any generation are always old and remain old in the eyes of their children, and the younger generation remains young in the eyes of their parents," Jirji remarked.

"What is wrong with *this* new generation, then? I mean, our children."

"Then the question is what's wrong with us, we, the older generation? Didn't we bring them into the world? Aren't we their parents? Aren't we responsible for their moral, religious, intellectual, and social wellbeing? Aren't we proud when they are good and successful? Why shouldn't we be ashamed of ourselves when they fail morally and professionally?" Jirji wondered.

"Let us not talk about the education of our children now," Nadim interjected, "we can do this later at a more convenient time. The urgent question is the next step in helping our children? This is our immediate responsibility."

"I agree with you, Nadim, but what kind of helpful strategies do you have in mind?"

"Do you mean we can resort to illegal or if necessary immoral strategies?" Jirji intervened. "I was and remain strongly opposed to any immoral or illegal strategy. We cannot, no matter the circumstance, violate the recognized legal and moral laws."

"But I think that we should pursue any strategy, legal or illegal, moral or immoral, as long as we can help them. They are our children. We are obligated to help them."

"Legal or illegal, moral or immoral strategies?" Jirji asked, his eyes wide.

"Any kind as long as we can help them."

"But is this the way of Orthodox Christians, of respectable citizens?"

"This is a practical matter, and our strategy should be practical."

"Do you mean the laws of the Christian church are not practical?"

"They are practical at home, in the church, and in certain types of friendships. But not in all cases."

"What types of cases are exceptions?"

"Those that promote our personal interests. The sphere of the practical is the sphere of personal interests. Any rule, method of action, or objective that promotes our personal interests is practical. This is the way of practical people, regardless of their religion, profession, or economic status. Show me one person around you or anywhere in the world who does not follow this way of thinking and behavior! On the other hand, show me a person who does not bend, twist, or break the laws of the state, the laws of your church, and the laws of your morality, if they obstruct the realization of one's interests. Even your priest, your educated people, and your politicians are willing to violate any kind of law if it stands in the way of their ambitions—of course, as discretely as possible." Nick, who was still in the grip of that cynical smile, stopped and focused his eyes on Jirji and then on Johannes. "We love you, Jirji. Every member of the family holds you in the highest esteem. But let me tell you that you are not a practical man. Your proper place is not this society as I said, before, but some monastery or ivory tower. What is the use of all your learning if you cannot live in this world? And how can you live in this world, if you do not live by the rules of practical life?"

"What if my personal interest is living according to the rules which originate from the depth of my mind as a human being?"

"Who told you that such an interest is practical? There are right and wrong personal interests. Those that promote your survival are practical."

"What kind of survival do you have in mind—human or material?"

"Survival! That's it!"

"Survival as an animal or as a human being?"

"Do you imply that the people around you, who work in the farms, factories, and in the offices of the different corporations and government agencies, and the people who clean the streets and public squares are not living as human beings?"

"What makes you a human being, Nick?"

"You are a trickster, Jirji. You are trying to make me say what I do not wish to say. I cannot compete with you in this game—"

"Let us continue this discussion another day," Nadim interjected, "our children are in prison. I have just heard that Faris was apprehended by the police a little while ago. What should we do?" He threw a glance at Jirji and continued, "I understand Jirji's emphasis on the need to respect the legal and moral rules of our society, but I also understand Nick's emphasis on the need to be practical. These two needs may not be reconcilable in our society at present, but I hope we can discover a course of action that recognizes both needs or at least avoids their undesirable consequences. This is our immediate responsibility."

"But what kind of help strategy should we adopt, then?" Nick asked.

"Jirji thinks we should let the law take its course," Abraham said. He argued that Faris and Bassam will most likely learn a good lesson from this devastating experience and hopefully will refrain from repeating the same crimes. He also discussed in some detail that it is our duty to respect the law of the state."

"But," Abraham emphasized, "What will the people say? What will the priest say? My son, Ibrahim, advised that this is our tough luck!"

"Please, Abraham, don't tell us what Ibrahim said or did not say! Everybody knows that he suffers from several psychological problems and requires psychotherapy. He is the laughing stock of our family. Our family doctor, who knows him very well, told me confidentially that he is delusional. When he speaks about fear or anger, he thinks that he is Sigmund Freud, when he speaks about the laws of motion, he thinks he is Isaac Newton, and when he speaks about the computer, he thinks he is Charles Babbage. He is convinced he is Mr. Know-it-all, and yet is a flunky. I really believe we should keep him out of this discussion."

"But he is my son," Abraham said, a note of anger evident in his voice.

"I thought you respected the truth." Abraham did not respond to this reminder. "My son should not be the subject of conversation. I refuse to talk about him. The question is what we should do now."

"We should identify the most influential officials in General Security and simply bribe them. Make sure that you approach them most tactfully. This means you should arrange the bribe in a way no one can discover," Nick recommended.

"Does this mean committing a crime to annul another crime?" Jirji interjected. "But, can one crime annul another crime?"

"Please, Jirji, keep your feet tethered to the ground of practical life," Nick said. "In practical life, what you call a crime is not a crime. It is a means of survival. How can you speak of crime when corruption is a way of life? No one can say that it is immoral to do one's best to survive!"

"Survive at any cost—of losing your dignity, your integrity, your honor, your humanity?"

"The world does not run by your moral and human values but by ambition, by a passion for life. Two of our sons are in prison. It is our duty to help them, and we should do all we can to help them!"

At this juncture of Nick's denunciation of Jirji's reaction to his recommendation, a soft knock was heard at the door. It stood ajar for a moment. Hanania's wife slipped it for a second and thrust a coded glance in Jeannette's direction. Jeannette deciphered its code and ran to the door. "The Sarkisians are here for a sympathy visit. Apparently, they know about the imprisonment of Bassam and Faris."

"Yes, they know almost everything."

"They are good friends. They are now paying their respects to Aunt Rachel and will be joining you shortly."

"Any bad news?" Nick asked when Jeannette returned to her chair. "Nothing but bad news these days," he said as he cast a strange look at Johannes.

"Why do you say 'bad'?" Hanania asked. "The Sarkisians are our dear friends. They always shared bad and good events with us."

"I say 'bad' because nothing but bad news seems to come our way at present. When the jinx pollutes a place with its ugly presence and bad odor, you can undoubtedly expect bad things to happen."

"What are you talking about? What jinx?"

The sardonic grin that surged on Nick's lips earlier reappeared in the same corners, but this time, he did not face Johannes only to avoid a possible confrontation with him. "Do you need more calamities to befall us to know that there is a jinx in our midst? If you try to connect the dots the way I did, you will see that they point to a jinx!" Hanania cast a very skeptical look at Nick but decided to avoid responding. But Jeanette was more skeptical than Hanania. "Is he hallucinating?" she wondered, "if not, he must be on the verge of some kind of hallucination." She pitied him.

"Uncle Nick, no one believes in jinxes these days."

"I do. Let me assure you that you will change your mind if or when you see one. You do not always recognize him, and let me emphasize that it is a he, not an it. He is a chameleon. He appears and does not appear at will, and he can assume any type of identity. But once you discover the logic of his tactics, you will be able to recognize him, no matter where or how he appears. You should delve deep into his soul to see the evil that dwells there."

This cryptic response was marginalized by a few soft knocks at the door. It was opened and revealed the presence of Yuri, Armen, and Tina. Yuri sat next to Johannes, Armen next to Hanania, and Tina next to Jeannette. "We were deeply saddened when we heard of Bassam's and Faris's imprisonment," Yuri said, addressing the three cousins, "Please, let me know if I can be of any help."

"Faris and Bassam need help, and we have been trying to find a way to help them. Any suggestions from you, Armen, and you, Tina, will be greatly appreciated." Nick said.

"By the way, Uncle Nick," Tina said, changing the subject, "I shall be delighted to answer any question you might have about law, freedom, and justice after I complete my graduate studies—"

"Graduate studies?" Nick interrupted her.

"Yes, I am now corresponding with the universities of Paris and London."

"Why not the University of Hamburg or Munich?" Nick responded with a sarcastic tone in his voice.

"Maybe, if Johannes recommends the right university for me." This last statement landed on Nick's ears the way a plume of lava falls on an orchard grove and rumples it.

"For goodness sake, not Germany!" Nick returned in the most desperate tone you can imagine.Although it was clear to everyone that Cupid's arrow had already found its way to Johannes's heart and baptized it with the fire that was burning in Tina's heart, still, Nick was hopeful that Faris might marry Tina. The possibility of a serious relationship between Tina and Johannes was not only a loathsome but also a crushing idea. The mere entertainment of this idea was, for Nick, a sacrilege.

"This should be the worst place in the universe. Besides, I doubt that your parents will allow you to study anywhere outside Latakia," Nick said, and turning his attention toward Tina's parents added, "Would you?"

"Tina is older than eighteen. She is an educated woman. She can make her own decisions. Her mother and I have no objection to any decision she makes as long as it is her decision."

Nick did not expect this kind of answer from Yuri. He felt that some demonic force was acting against him and the whole Mitya family, that Johannes was the living embodiment of this force, and that it was his duty to combat it.

Although Tina was dressed in black, out of respect for Abraham and Hanania and their families, and although she did not wear any makeup for the same reason, she was a radiant image of feminine beauty. This radiance did not escape Nick's eyes mainly because he was hoping that she was going to be his daughter-in-law and because he firmly believed that Johannes was a formidable challenge to his son. This belief was now shaken a little because his son committed a criminal act and because he might spend some time in prison. He was under the vague impression that the Sarkisians were close friends of the family and that Yuri and Armen would not object to a romantic alliance between Tina and Faris. Wasn't he Tina's favorite uncle? The notion that Johannes might be a real and most likely a stronger suitor than Faris for Tina crossed his mind, but he dismissed it because he thought that he would be able to eliminate Johannes either by scaring him away or by liquidating him if he had to. No one will stop Faris from marrying Tina, he felt. Oh, how human beings can rationalize their way out of their most destructive desires and foolish dreams.

But the radiance that captivated Johannes's eyes was pure, innocent, natural, and enchanting. Johannes delighted in the enchantment, and he wished he could linger in it forever. Although he was not aware of it, he was falling in love with the soul behind the radiance! It is strange how men and women sometimes do not know that they are falling in love, or that they have already fallen in love until they relish its sweetness, its elegance, and its charm, and until they are smitten by it for good! How can you enjoy it if you are not in it? But what is stranger, is that when you relish this sweetness and this charm, when you delight in its infinite warmth, you undergo a gradual, inner transformation without even noticing it; and when this happens to you, you begin to see differently, feel differently, and act differently, of course from the standpoint of the enchantment you are in. You begin to see yourself and the world around through the eyes of your beloved—with her tender, elegant, and enchanting mind and heart. How can it be otherwise if you see the world and yourself through her eyes? Does this mean that when this happens to you, you lose your own mind and heart—your identity? Of course not! You gain a new, richer mind and heart, and a richer identity. But, alas, is it possible for this kind of enchantment to take place from one side only? No, because it is impossible to feel, and especially to be in it, if it is not desirable and welcoming by the enchanter. Human enchantment is dialogical in nature. How can you feel its infinite warmth if you are not transported on its wings to the heart of the enchanter? Unfortunately, most, if not all, of the beauty we encounter in the market place of social life is made-up beauty. It can be pleasant, sensuous, even titillating, but not charming. Only human beauty, the kind that radiates from the human heart, can be charming. This kind of beauty is the true language of the heart.

Although Tina did not notice the charm of her radiant beauty, for she could not, she noticed the elegance of Johannes's look; she saw the radiance of its charm, she felt it, and she welcomed it into her heart. People are eager to hear about miracles and to witness them, if possible, but they can hardly see, much less contemplate, the miracle of love—the moment in which two hearts are clasped in an eternal embrace. And they can barely see, much less feel, the fire it generates in the loving heart.

"Love—miraculous?" You wonder. Yes, love is miraculous. "And why," you ask. Because when two souls, each of which is a world of thoughts, feelings, emotions, aspirations, desires, interests, experiences, are fused into one, when they become one, and yet become more magnificent in their two-ness, in their individualities the earth under their feet trembles and the wind carries them to the depth of the infinite and the sun over their head dances on its rays to the music of the divine. If this is not the most wondrous miracle the human mind can imagine, please, let me know what it may be!

Nick witnessed the effulgence of this miracle. Although he should have celebrated it, he hated it. He was seething with fury, the kind that borders on madness, and he cursed it with the flames of his hatred. He wished he could stop or in some way, undermine it. "How can this jinx spirit away my future daughter-in-law from me?" He asked silently in the heat of this fury. "Tina," he said, "my cousins and I need your help!" Nick was known for surprises, but not for dramatic surprises. This time he was successful in creating a suspenseful situation.

"My help?" Tina responded with curious eyes. Abraham and Nadim frowned and looked at each other. Yuri and Armen looked at each other and then at Tina.

"Yes, we have been discussing the best way to help Bassam and Faris. Let me at once say that our nephews are good young men. I tend to think they simply made a mistake, one we are trying to mend. Unfortunately, they are in prison. I am calling on your assistance only because, as a specialist in political science, you must be knowledgeable in the ways of the law. A person like you should be able to voice an opinion on a practical matter that relates to the law."

"Are you sure, Uncle Nick?"

"Absolutely! Can a person justifiably bribe a government official to free two young men from prison? The issue is whether we can let Bassam and possibly Faris languish and rot in prison for several years or forever, which is worse than hell. Is losing Bassam for the sake of the law worth it? We love our nephews. We feel a strong obligation to help them. Can we be justified in bribing some government officials to free them from prison? I tend to think that bribing some officials, most of whom are poor and can hardly support their families in order to free them on the grounds that they would earn some money they urgently need, that the state would not be harmed, and that the young men would return safe and sound to their families is justifiable. What is more important—life or the law? What makes this question hard for us is that it is debatable. The law of our state is guarded by corrupt judges and lawyers. Every one of them uses the law as a means to personal advantage. Law has become a commodity. Its salespersons are none other its guardians! Jirji recommended that we do not bribe anybody or resort to illegal means to free them. I have given my view. What do you think?"

"Wow, Uncle Nick! I cannot answer this question. I am only a student. You should pose it to Johannes. He is a university doctor. The government is one of his areas of expertise. Justice is his preeminent interest."

The mere mention of Johannes's name sent shivers through Nick's body. "Him? The—," he almost shouted. "But he is practically a foreigner. He does not know our laws, and he does not know the inner dynamics of our government, of how it works."

"It may come as a surprise if I tell you that Johannes does not only know about the inner structure and dynamics of the German government, he also knows about the structure and inner dynamics of many countries of the world, especially the Syrian government. He knows about us more than we know about ourselves. He does not have to live here to know about the institutions which govern the different dimensions of our lives." Tina stopped for a second and continued, "Uncle Nick, the law is law everywhere; its purpose is one and the same everywhere. Human nature is one and the same everywhere. There are good and bad people everywhere. There are lovable and despicable people everywhere. Some people are corrupt, and others are not everywhere. Some people are law-abiding citizens, and some are not everywhere."

Tina's parents, who witnessed their daughter express herself so articulately, so conversantly, were simply astonished. An expression of pride emanated from Armen's face, but she suppressed it only to avoid the possible charge of siding with her daughter against Nick. She and her husband remained silent. Abraham and Nadim covered their faces with twin expressions of bafflement. Jeannette, who was sitting next to Tina, pinched her thigh and stifled a smile that was eager to grip her lips. Johannes, who was still sizzling in the radiance of her beauty, was blushing, and the blush that adorned his cheeks was visible, particularly to Nick.

The Mitya citadel cannot, and should not, fall! Nick was willing to fight for it to the death against subversives like Johannes and liberals like Yuri, but especially against Johannes, who was about to steal his future daughter-in-law from him. He brushed aside the thought, even the possibility that his cousins and other members of the family might not agree with him or support him in his contest against liberals and subversives. He knew he was right! Anyway, does it matter who supports you in this kind of contest if you know you are right?

"What do you think, Johannes?" Tina asked. Alas, Johannes's capacity of thinking was out of commission. How can you think, at least clearly, when you are sizzling in the fire of love, when this fire is still raging in your mind and heart, and when the enchanter that sparked that fire is asking you a question about something that pales into insignificance compared to the grandeur of this fire? Johannes was living a precious moment. What are the ideas to life? No matter their significance or greatness, ideas remain silent when life flourishes in our minds and hearts. But love is resourceful. Love is the son of the god of resource, after all! The blush that was flaming on his cheeks imperceptibly moved to Tina's cheeks, and the two fires that were raging in their hearts and minds were locked in a momentary, yet eternal, embrace. This embrace lingered. Everyone present in that room witnessed it! Armen delighted in it, so did Jeannette and Yuri. Abraham and Hanania were indifferent to it, but Nick was enraged by it. He could not stand it. With the impatience of a jealous teenager, Nick repeated Tina's question, "What do you think, Johannes?" He pursed his lips so tightly, even Armen noticed the sudden change in his temper. She felt sorry for the man. Regardless of whether they are an enemy or a friend, a defeated person is always pathetic. They arouse a feeling of pity in our hearts.

As if emerging from a reverie, as if making a sudden move from the divine to the secular, Johannes stared at Nick and said, "If you want to know about my reaction to the possibility that Tina may do her graduate studies in Germany or anywhere else, it is simple: I think it is an excellent idea, and I shall do all I can to assist her in choosing the right university. I am confident that she will distinguish herself as an outstanding scholar in the field of political science. Waste is sinful. Impeding the human mind from growing and developing its potential is the greatest kind of waste, therefore, the greatest sin we can commit in this world."

"Is this the judgment of a scholar or of a man in quest of a love adventure? We have a large herd of Casanovas in our society; they litter the streets and alleys of Latakia. They have developed a cult of their own. Our people have become experts in the ways, aims, and tricks of this cult." This uncalled-for response from Nick aroused a flurry of subdued "hums," heaving chests, and "wows." Many eyes vacillated between Nick's and Johannes's faces.

When you are relishing the fire of love, when you are at the mercy of its flames, you become a spring of love. And, if you happen to be a loving human being, the spring you become flows from your heart like a river. Such a river is divine! Do you know that this kind of heart can neither see nor do evil, no matter its kind?

"Uncle Nick, the judgment I made was the judgment of a scholar. It was objective."

"How can you explain the fire that is oozing, yes, oozing from of your cheeks, then? How can you explain the possibility of an objective judgment that springs from a man touched by the finger of Eros? Did someone mention to you that this god is a frequent visitor to the streets of Latakia?"

"Has it occurred to you, dear Uncle, that genuine love does not confuse or jumble the mind but makes it lucid, sharpens its logical powers, and inclines it to love the truth and seek it? A lover can be poor, oppressed, and alienated, but they can never abandon the dedication to the truth. Show me a romantic lover, and I show you a truth lover. Can a lover shy away from objective judgment, regardless of how painful or strenuous the situation might be?"

"And now," Nick intervened, "since, as you say, you are a lover of the truth, since you are an authority on the nature and aims of government, and since you know so much about our society, let me remind you of the central question of our conversation: Can we be justified in bribing government officials or in resorting to illegal means to free our nephews from prison?"

"I remember the question, and I remember the reasons which led to it. Let me first remark that this question did not arise from philosophical reflection but from a deep love for Faris and Bassam, which commands the highest of our respect for you and also for Uncles Abraham, Hanania, and Jirji. Any question that does not arise from a loving heart is an impotent question. I assure you, Uncle Nick, that I profoundly share your agony and the torment this tragic course of events has created. My heart aches for the family, and I am willing to shoulder the burden of this tragedy.

"But although this calamity is devastating, I tend to agree with Jirji that it would be wrong to violate the law or to resort to illegal means to free your nephews. He is the kind of mind that thinks carefully, logically, and critically, and he would not express an opinion unless it is buttressed by a valid line of reasoning. I shall be glad to offer arguments in support of his judgment. It is better to bear the affliction of one injustice than the affliction of more than one injustice. But I think that we must respect the law, no matter the consequences."

"Do you have children, Johannes?" Everyone looked aghast at Nick when he asked this question, for it ostensibly implied that Nick assumed that he was married and had children in Germany. People in Latakia and other Syrian cities know that some foreigners who came to Syria alone for a limited period were married and had children. Many of them felt a strong need for female companionship during their stay; they presented themselves as bachelors and so were able to get married. They abandoned their Syrian wives when they returned to their homeland. However, Jirji, Nadim, and perhaps the Sarkisians, thought that Nick's purpose in posing the question was to embarrass Johannes and, if possible, to smear his character. But this was not Nick's purpose, even though he strongly desired to humiliate and anger him. But Johannes was not embarrassed or in any way offended. It is hard for an innocent man to be ashamed or offended in a situation like this one. He was simply puzzled. He hesitated a little only because the puzzlement was acute and because he was groping for the right words to express himself. He stared at Nick for a moment to determine if he were serious. But Nick was very serious, and he waited for an answer to his question. Nick demanded an explanation: "Answer the question!" Nick was a man on a mission, and his mission was to show that bribing officials to free his nephews was a justifiable practice, at least in Latakia. "Answer the question!" Nick demanded again when he noticed that Johannes was still hesitating about answering the question.

"No, I do not have children."

"Then you have never been a father?"

"No."

"You see, dear Johannes, you do not know what it means to be a father, and you do not know what fatherly love is. A father does not see the law when he sees his son tortured, when he sees him die a hundred deaths every day in a hellish prison, and he does not see your justice or any other type of justice when he knows that a corrupt society and a corrupt legal establishment create the conditions for young men and women to be immoral or criminals. Does your existing law care about the conditions that produce corrupt young people? Is a legal system that does not create the conditions of respecting it a good system? The heart of a loving father cares! Love is the measure of justice, not the law of your corrupt politicians. We love our children. I ask you, Jirji, and you, Tina, to step from your ivory towers down into the realm of reality. You should always remember that any law that does not provide the conditions for the development of the moral behavior of its citizens in this or any other society is a bad law. Am I under obligation to obey a bad law? I still remember a conversation I had with an old monk a few years ago. He made a distinction between moral law and human law. He argued that moral law is superior to human law and that it should be the source and foundation of human law. He also said, this time ironically, that the essence of moral law is love. I am not in a position to ascertain whether this view is true, but it seems to carry a reasonable measure of truth, I think."

"I follow your line of reasoning," Johannes replied, "but it is hard to defend it on both theoretical and practical levels—"

"It may be objectionable on a theoretical level, but on a practical level?"

"Yes, on both levels. The sources and validity of both moral and human laws are some of the most complicated, contested, and challenging questions in both philosophy and political science."

"I recommend," Abraham intervened, "that we defer this most informative conversation to this evening or perhaps next week. Supper will be served shortly. It would, I think, be good to have a drink now. I shall need your help in the kitchen, Jeannette," he added.

"I shall come too, Uncle Abraham," Tina suggested.

Nick suddenly stood and sprinted to the kitchen immediately after Abraham left the room. He stood next to Abraham and said in a whisper, "I need to see you for a second." Abraham threw a strange look at his cousin and whispered back, "Now?"

"Yes, now. Just a second!" Nick repeated.

Abraham entrusted the young women with the task of preparing the drinks and followed Nick to the veranda. "Yesterday, hours before he was apprehended by the police, apparently when he was meeting with some drug dealers, Faris spotted you with your mistress, Nina, at the Mukhtar Café. He asked me to warn you to be careful. We do not need another scandal, Abraham, not now— just be careful!" Abraham did not say a word. He was already suffering pangs of guilt over his son's imprisonment, and now he? He closed his eyes so hard, his eyelids almost sank into their sockets. Under the heavyweight of a crushing frown on his brow, he remained transfixed in place for a few minutes.

In the meantime, Jeannette and Tina were having their own conversation in the kitchen. "He loves you! I told you he does! Don't lose him! He is a godsend. You will never meet a real man in this city."

Jeannette said in a hardly audible voice.

"But I love him, Jeannette! Something magical happened between us when we first met. He is handsome, he is elegant in the way he speaks and behaves, but I do not think that his beauty or elegance is what attracted me to him; it is something else, something more profound, more powerful, more fascinating, more irresistible than either beauty or grace. I was able to see it and feel it, but I am unable to describe it. It was more like an aura that radiated from his face, from the way he spoke, from what he said, especially the way he looked at me. Oh, Jeannette, his eyes spoke the language of a special kind of magic. This aura was enchanting, and I was enchanted. I could not resist it! I am absolutely confident that he felt the same way about me. It was like some mysterious power that opened our hearts to each other! It felt like a warm breeze enfolded me and squeezed me and kept squeezing me. It was a mysterious squeeze, because the tighter it became, the more I desired it, and the more I desired, the more I desired to remain within its folds"

"You are in love, Tina! How does it feel to be in love?"

"I feel like I am in heaven—" this intimate conversation was interrupted by Abraham.

"Why don't you take the drinks to the living room?"

"Go ahead, take the drinks. I shall bring the appetizers in a minute." Jeannette said to Tina.

"A sip of araq is what I need now," Nick said when Tina appeared with the tray of araq glasses. He took a gulp and blurted out: "This araq is excellent. I do not remember drinking anything like this in my life!"

"It was made by my father," Hanania said.

"You mean Uncle Mikhail?"

"Yes. He learned the secret of araq brewing from his great grandfather, the progenitor of this whole family. They say that my father was his favorite grandson. My father learned many skills from him. My great grandfather even sent him to the College of Military Science in Istanbul."

"Your father?" Johannes asked, interrupting Hanania, "I never knew this."

"Yes, and many other facts, not many people know about him. My father was a highly educated man. He always pretended he was ignorant, but you had to poke him hard in a conversation to glean the depth of his knowledge. Many people think he was a sot, but they did not know that he was the kindest man on earth. His heart was made of tenderness. He was especially good to me. He always gave me a secret allowance when I was young. 'Buy Baklava or something you like,' he used to say when he gave me the allowance, and he secretly put some money in my pocket when I grew older."

This confessional revelation, which must have come as a surprise to some ears in the room, was discontinued by Abraham's sudden appearance. He took his araq glass, raised it a little, and said, "I would like to welcome cousin Johannes to our home. I wish you a pleasant and successful stay in Latakia, Johannes!"

"I am fortunate to be in your presence," Johannes stood and said, "to meet my cousins and their families, and to get acquainted with my cultural roots," and looking in Tina's direction, he continued, "I have a strong feeling that the sun of my real life began to shine here in Latakia." He stopped, swallowed his saliva, because his throat was dry, and emphasized, "No person in this land is as fortunate as I am." A soft smile graced his lips when he sat down.

Nick did not like what he heard and what he saw, not because what he heard and saw was bad or ugly, and not because it was true or false, but because Johannes stood at the door of a truth he never expected. That door was abruptly opened, and a flood of questions began to flow into his mind. Every word Hanania said seemed to corroborate and indeed shed ample light on Mikhail's confession to Johannes. But neither Abraham nor Hanania knew about Mikhail's disclosure. What if they knew? What if the whole family knew? "Am I, Faris and his family, my daughter, Bassam and his family, yes indeed the entire family, paying for the sins we have committed against Uncle Mikhail?" Nick thought in the silence of his recondite soul. "Should Abraham know the truth? Should he and the family know that Aunt Rachel is not the saint she has purported to be all these years? Haven't we, the Mitya family, killed Uncle Mikhail? Aren't we responsible for his miserable life and death? How did this so-called matriarch manage to deceive the whole family about the evil she committed against her good husband? Oh, no, Johannes is not the jinx of the Mitya family! The jinx is Aunt Rachel!"

This flood of questions was arrested by Hanania's wife: "Please, dinner is served. I hope you enjoy the stuffed grape leaves and raw kibbe!" She halted her speech only because tears were rolling over her cheeks and flowing into the corners of her mouth. She wiped them with a small towel stuck to her waist and added, "May God rest his soul in peace! Uncle Mikhail used to like these dishes very much. I hope you like them, Johannes!" She left as soon as she uttered "Johannes," mainly because the tears began to roll over her cheeks again.

Everyone in the room saw the tears and felt the love that gave rise to them. Nick, who had been oblivious to Jameela's existence during the past years, mostly because Aunt Rachel kept her in the kitchen most of the time, and on the fringe of family life, did not only see and feel but also understood their meaning. The world of truth, Aunt Rachel craftily veiled, which began to crack at the coffin of Uncle Mikhail a few days ago, was utterly disclosed at Abraham's and Hanania's dining table. Nick saw, heard, and understood the whole truth at that very table! He hurled a look at Hanania, who was sitting at the right of the table, sipping his araq, then at Abraham, who was placing a roll of grape leaves in his mouth, then at Aunt Rachel, who sat next to Abraham eating raw kibbe. He contemplated those faces for a few moments, and he contemplated the magnitude of the crime Aunt Rachel had committed. It became clear to him, clear as crystal that Hanania was a bastard, but he was also the true son of his father, Mikhail, the father who loved him truly more than any of the men in the family. Whether by intuition, by the kind of attitude Hanania assumed toward his father, or the by the way Mikhail behaved toward Hanania, Jameela knew that her husband was Mikhail's favorite son and that she was his favorite daughter-in-law. She loved him as her real father.

When you discover or even stumble on a significant truth when you see it in the fullness of its light, you cannot ignore it, you cannot remain silent, and you feel compelled to act according to its precepts and implications. You feel an urge to right a wrong, regardless of whether it was done by us. For some mysterious reason, you feel this obligation irrespective of whether you act or refrain from acting according to it. Do we not feel guilty, at least tense, when we do not act according to it? Do we not feel guilty when we violate a moral rule or intuition? Do we not feel inner satisfaction when we perform our duties?

Although the agony of suffering over the elopement of his daughter with a Durzi and the imprisonment of his nephews was aflame in the depth of his soul, Nick experienced a feeling of inner peace, of relief, of catharsis. He wished he could leap toward Johannes and Jirji and kiss them, but he could not, not out of embarrassment, for he was known for his courage and determination, but out of respect for the light that shone in his mind and soul. Who could have grasped the meaning of that light, but Johannes and Jirji? Who could have understood the mystery of that miraculous light—its majesty, inner power, and the kind of joy it creates in the human soul? Unawares, Nick raised his araq glass and said, "May we have a toast in honor of the late Uncle Mikhail?" Everyone sitting at the table, except Abraham and Aunt Rachel, raised their glasses, some filled with araq and others with water or beer, and in unison said, "To his good memory!" Tears filled Johannes's eyes! He understood more than anyone in the Mitya family the kind of transformation Nick was undergoing, but he did not understand the power of love that was flowing from his heart!

Nick did not notice that Abraham and Aunt Rachel declined his proposal to honor Mikhail's memory. Indeed, the idea of who did or did not honor his Uncle's memory did not cross his mind. Should this social technicality matter? Should he know how they or anyone else felt about it? Do you worry about how people feel or think when you stand in the light of the truth? This light is empowering: it inspires courage, understanding, and it enlivens the sense of beauty, goodness, and compassion in our minds and hearts. Nick was ready and willing to confront any person about the way he acted. "Uncle Mikhail was a good man," he said. He gulped one more sip of araq. Johannes thrust a look of amazement, of compassion, at Nick. He wished he could hug him! He could not. Nonetheless, his wish was transformed into a smile of love!

Although he was unable to unlock the secret of Nick's sudden change in behavior, Johannes understood, and he welcomed it. Impulsively, Jirji, who was puzzled by the same shift, and more amazed than puzzled, the way his German cousin was, looked intently at Johannes. Their eyes met; they understood each other. Tina, whose eyes hardly left Johannes's face, noticed this mysterious exchange between Johannes and Jirji. She was not curious about its content. Seeing the man she loved happy was all she desired.

"You are not eating, Johannes," Jameela said, "how do you like the kibbe?" She was not aware of the smiles that were flying between Jirji and Johannes and between Tina and her beloved across the table. But Johannes was able to hear his aunt.

"Wonderful, Aunt! Please be patient with me. I was eating it as an appetizer with my araq. I shall delve into the stuffed grape leaves and kefta momentarily."

"This is how Uncle Mikhail used to eat his kibbe."

"And this is how my grandfather used to eat it."

Nick was so happy, so excited, so elated, he could not linger at that table anymore. He cast a glance at his wife and nodded, then he stood up. He and his wife expressed their appreciation for an excellent and beautiful evening. "I look with anticipation to seeing you next Sunday, Johannes." He shook Jirji's hand warmly and pressed it hard. "Yes," he said, "you are the treasure of this family. He moved closer to him and hugged him. He was joyful. Jirji welcomed his hug. He felt what Johannes felt!

Although he was convinced that Aunt Rachel committed the capital crime of the century, although he decided to keep it a secret, and although he was convinced that Abraham knew that his brother Hanania was a bastard, he thanked Abraham for a wonderful evening. Contrary to the family custom, he kissed Aunt Rachel three times on her cheeks and wished her good health and long life. His heart was overflowing with compassion. He walked to the other side of the table where Jameela was sitting and said to her, "Thank you, Jameela. The kibbe and the kefta were truly delicious. But you, yes, you, Jameela, are the best!" Abraham was watching Nick communicating his feelings to Jameela with open eyes and mouth. Neither he nor any of the family members, except Jirji and Johannes, had an inkling of what prompted Nick to express himself the way he did.

Most people tend to think that the most significant miracles happen in nature or social life. But it is reasonable to say as I did earlier that the only sphere we can, and should, look for them is the sphere of the human heart, and the only type of miracle that happens in this sphere is the miracle of love. This is the type of miracle that was happening not only in Nick's heart but also in Tina's and Johannes's hearts that night.

Johannes spent the night dreaming of his beloved, and Tina spent it at home with the warmth Johannes left in her heart.

SEVEN

Love Between Tina and Johannes Blossoms

ONE OF THE TRADITIONS of the Mitya family, which Nick observed scrupulously, was what he called "Sunday Dinner." It was hosted by one of the cousins. Sunday was a day of rest, and it was a family day. In the morning, the families attended church, while in the afternoon, they enjoyed the most sumptuous meal of the week, after which they took a walk on the cornice soon after they had their siesta. The children always looked forward to their allowance and sweets, the women visited and reviewed the news and gossip of the week, and the men discussed the main problems of the family, the state of the business market, and the most recent political scandals. The Sarkisians were always invited to these dinners. They were the closest friends and confidants of the Mityas. Yuri, who chaired the department of education in the district of Latakia, was the most abundant source of advice to the older and younger generations of the family, to the extent that the young people called him "Uncle Yuri." He was known for his erudition, wisdom, and moral integrity.

On the following Sunday, dinner was hosted by Nick and his wife. Aunt Rachel and her son Abraham and his wife did not come to dinner that Sunday. "We are still grieving for my father," he said to Nick. "Besides, we are painfully worried about Bassam's imprisonment. We have to find a way to free him from that cursed prison or at least reduce his sentence to a few years, if possible." Nick thought that Abraham's excuse for declining dinner that Sunday was lame, unjustifiable because he was still suffering over the elopement of his daughter to a Durzi and Nadim over the imprisonment of his son, Faris. He did not contest Abraham's refusal only because he did not wish to argue with him. "It is impossible to converse, much less argue with a petrified mind," Nick reasoned. He always felt that the blood that flowed in Abraham's veins was not a Mitya but Airanji blood—the blood of his mother's side of the family.

The Sarkisians arrived at Nick's house a little earlier than usual on that Sunday because Armen's help was urgently needed in the kitchen. Preparing a Sunday meal for a large family was a demanding undertaking. Armen and Tina streamed into the kitchen the moment they arrived at Nick's house. Yuri joined Nick in the living room. Deema was already in the kitchen. She was stuffing squash and eggplant with rice and meat when Armen and Tina arrived in the kitchen. "Where is Jirji?" Armen asked Deema.

"He went to Bouqa to fetch Johannes." Sparks of excitement flew from Tina's eyes when she heard this response. But those sparks did not fly only from her eyes; they also flew from her beautiful face. It seemed that the black dress she was wearing that Sunday was designed by Aphrodite herself. It caught Deema's and Nora's attention. "You look exquisite in this dress!" Deema remarked.

"My mother made it," Tina replied with a feeling of pride.

"You will be an object of envy today, my dear." Tina smiled without responding to this comment.

Jeannette was thrilled to see her friend dressed so elegantly. She embraced Tina warmly and asked her to stand by her side and watch her prepare the appetizers. "But I wish to help!" Tina whispered.

"Today is your day," Jeannette whispered back teasingly, "You are excused from work, no one knows, you may break some saucers—no one knows!"

"Oh, Jeannette!"

"I wish you'd break some saucers!" Jeannette mumbled. But Tina heard the mumble!

"But can I be in charge of the araq?"

"Only if you promise not to drop the glasses!"

Jeannette was right. Every time there was a knock at the front door, or whenever the door was opened or closed, Tina would twitch a little and look to see who was coming in. She was anxious. When you are in love, especially when you are waiting for your beloved, your sense of time rumples. It becomes elastic, and sometimes it fractures. The second becomes a minute, the minute an hour, the hour a day, and the day a week. You wish you can jump over the stream of time, short or long, and land in your lover's presence, embrace them and feel the warmth you have been waiting for ever since you were in your mother's womb. But waiting is painful because it creates a state of restlessness. However, the waiting of the lover for their beloved is sweet. She prefers to wait for him and suffers the anxiety of restlessness rather than do anything else. By some miraculous force, she tolerates it and transforms it into a desirable pain. Why not, if the imminent future that unfolds in her consciousness is suffused with the presence of her beloved? Love is a miracle, and it is miraculous!

Impulsively, Tina sprinted to the front door the instant she heard Johannes's voice. Yuri was still welcoming Jirji and Johannes when she stood next to her father. A mysterious feeling inclined her to move closer to Johannes and kiss him, and she wished to linger in the love of that kiss forever. But that feeling was stifled because men and women were not allowed to kiss in public. Nevertheless, the warmth of that feeling spread to her cheeks and then and covered them with a lovely blush. Tina did not wear rouge that day, but the blush she wore at that moment was a reflection of the fire that was flaming in her heart and on her lips. Johannes noticed it and moved closer to her. "Welcome!" She said in a most alluring voice. It rose from the depth of her heart and flowed into Johannes's as the sweetest drop of nectar!

"Oh, Tina—" he whispered. He could not complete his sentence only because he did not wish anyone to intrude into the privacy of their hearts. He moved closer to her and said with a trembling whisper, "I have been racing with time all week long! If only you know how many times I wished I could fly from Bouqa to your house! If only you know how many times I wished I could knock at your bedroom window, place my heart at its sill, and fly back to Bouqa incognito! Oh, how I wish I could listen to the beats of your heart, to the music of those beats! Oh, how time is cruel!" Johannes withdrew a little from her and looked into her eyes with a shy smile. Although Nick, Yuri, and Jirji were exchanging some remarks about the imprisonment of Faris and Bassam, they felt the fire of the love that was crackling in Johannes's and Tina's hearts, and although silently, they blessed it and wished it to remain alive. It was an awkward moment for them because they did not like to snoop on the privacy of that fire. They felt an urge to leave the lovers alone. "Let us move to the living room!" Nick suggested.

And the lovers were left alone in that entrance. Their eyes were clasped in a tender, yet passionate, conversation; they spontaneously moved closer to each other and allowed their lips to sizzle in the heat of a kiss. Oh, how sweet, how divine, was that kiss! Johannes embraced Tina with his strong, youthful arms and pressed her tightly to his chest. But, unfortunately, that precious moment did not last long! A knock at the door sundered them from each other but united them in a moment of embarrassment. Instinctively, Johannes dashed to the kitchen to greet the ladies, and Tina walked slowly to the door and opened it. Nadim, Hanania, and their wives appeared at the door. Contrary to their faces, which exuded sadness, Tina's glowed with warmth and cheerfulness. She hugged Jameela and Sarah and led them to the kitchen. The men proceeded to the living room. When Tina and her guests were approaching the kitchen door, Johannes was leaving it. He greeted them and joined the men in the living room.

It is difficult for people to act deliberately, or even commonsensically, when they are caught in an embarrassing situation or when they are surprised by an unexpected occurrence. But sometimes the in-built system of the self-defense mechanism circumvents it. Nick and Yuri understood the dynamics of Johannes's and Tina's rendezvous and shielded them.

"Any news about Bassam and Faris?" Yuri asked when Nadim and Hanania had taken their chairs.

"Jirji should answer this question," Nadim replied. Yuri cast an inquiring look at Jirji and waited for an answer.

"I have met twice with a lawyer I respect and trust. After a lengthy discussion of several options, we've reached the conclusion that our aim should be to transform Faris's prison sentence to 'monetary punishment' with the proviso that he would not repeat the same offense or any other type of legal offence. This condition was added because this is not the first time Faris was apprehended for money black marketeering. The lawyer thinks that this is the most hopeful option."

"I think this a laudable opportunity—what do you think, Hanania?"

"I really like it."

"And you, Nadim?" Yuri asked.

"I welcome it. For me, my son's health and safety are more important than anything in the world."

"You see," Hanania added, "if you bribe General Security officials, they think they own you. They will constantly come to your store and ask you for a gift or some kind of favor. They are nasty leeches."

"Were you able to discuss Bassam's case with the lawyer, Jirji?" Yuri asked.

"Yes, we discussed his case. The lawyer's immediate reaction is that his case is recalcitrant. Bassam killed a young man. Formally, this is a capital crime. But they will not treat it as premeditated murder, mainly because he killed him by accident and because he was under the influence of drugs when he killed him. Still, no one else killed him. In fact, I discussed this option at length with the lawyer. He thinks that our best strategy is to aim at a reduced sentence. He thinks that if Bassam exemplifies good behavior, his sentence might be reduced accordingly. He cannot give us a final opinion at present, but this is the general plan of action he proposed. If we agree to it, he can begin work on this case immediately." Nick was listening carefully to Jirji's account with a stiff frown on his brow. He looked at Jirji and then at Yuri with languishing, droopy eyes. It was clear to everyone in the room that he was in torment over the plight he and his cousins were suffering.

What can you do as a father when your son commits a capital crime? You can feel guilty—so what? You can revolt against your family, against society, against Fate, and against God—so what? To what end? You might change your way of thinking and act as a father, but you cannot change the legal establishment. All you can do is submit to the facts because neither you nor anyone can change them, and do the best you can. Jirji's account of the options recommended by the lawyer revealed the truth of the present predicament. Nick looked at his cousins and said, "Let it be!"

"But that is not all!" Jirji continued. All the eyes in the room were fixed on his face. "I think, and with the approval of the lawyer, a statement of apology drafted by the lawyer and signed in the presence of a notary public should be sent to the parents of the young man Bassam killed. This letter should emphasize that Bassam was in a brawl with their son and that he did not intend to kill him."

"What!" Nick almost shouted.

"Yes, and I advise you and your wife, Nadim, to pay a friendly visit to the bereaved parents and condole them. You should stress to them that what your son did was wrong, that it was against your values and beliefs about life, and that you feel remorse about your son's criminal act."

"Is this visit a kind of bribe?" Nick snapped.

"Not at all! It is the right thing to do, and it is the human thing to do. If Bassam killed a human being involuntarily, he should feel guilty and express sorrow for his actions. Bassam is responsible for what he did even if what he did was *in* and not *because* of ignorance. Is this too much to ask?"

"Are you serious?"

"Very serious!"

"Are you realistic?" Nick said, poking Jirji one more time.

"Doing the right thing is always realistic!"

"Always?"

"Yes, on the condition that it is done wisely. Remember: Violence breeds violence, hate breeds hate." Jirji stopped and frowned and stared into the empty corner of the room that faced him.

"Why don't you say it, Jirji?" Nick ejaculated.

"Say what?" Jirji responded with a blank face.

"Say it, Jirji! Are you afraid to say that love does not always breed love, not always? Why don't you say it, Jirji? Oh, Jirji, does love always breed love? If love breeds love, our world would be heaven on earth."

"Those who love do not look backward and sideward. They do not expect any kind of reward for what they do. They always look forward. They love because their hearts are fountains of love. They act according to the kind of fountain they are! There is a mine of love in your heart, Nick. Listen to the voice of your heart."

"I sometimes think, Jirji, that you are not a Mitya! You must be cut from a different cloth."

"I am a Mitya just like you, and let me tell you that I am less perfect than any of the members of this family and all the people around us."

The araq tray Tina was carrying when she entered the room with Jeannette, who was carrying the appetizers tray, shook a little, and the glasses rattled a little. A subdued smile flitted on Tina's lips, and a bold smile danced on Jeannette's lips as the two ladies approached the Mitya cousins and Yuri. Tina was so flustered, she could not even glance at the man who charmed her heart. She simply lowered the araq tray and moved it closer to him. But he could not resist looking at her glowing face, and he could not refrain from sympathizing with her poignant fluster. His hand moved slowly, slug-gishly to the tray because his hand and his heart were not in sync. He held a glass without looking at it. It was difficult for him to remove his eyes off that glowing face. Although she avoided his eyes, she felt the warmth of his look, and she reveled in it. Oh, how wonderful it is when you know that you have spoken, you have communicated, and you have touched your beloved!

"Thank you!" She said when he removed his glass from the tray. She looked at him and smiled. "Enjoy it!"

"I shall not be drinking araq, I shall be drinking the sweetest nectar ever made by the gods," he whispered.

Nick noticed this tete-a-tete. "Why don't you and Jeannette join us, my dear?" He said when his cousins and Yuri were served their drinks and the appetizers placed on the make-shift side tables.

"We shall be happy to join you, Uncle Nick," Jeannette replied, although the question was addressed to Tina.

"It seems to me that you are developing a liking for araq," Nadim said to Johannes when the two young ladies left the room.

"Frankly, I am not a drinker, but I feel a desire to drink araq here in Latakia because I discovered that the event of sharing a drink with my cousins is a meaningful experience. It has a symbolic significance."

"What does it symbolize?"

"I may be mistaken, but I think it symbolizes the value of human community—of fellowship, mutual aid, human solidarity, and especially the joy of human presence. I enjoy the drink not because I feel a need for it but because the occasion of drinking it is meaningful."

"I have never heard this kind of explanation before," Nick remarked.

"But having a drink induces a feeling of liberation. One feels free, relaxed when drinking."

"But this is a false feeling of liberation because it is short-lived and, most of the time, unrealistic, if not irrational. It is tantamount to a flight from reality. It does not solve any problems; on the contrary, it prolongs them and frequently complicates them."

"Why don't you sit, my dear?" Nick said when the two ladies entered the living room. "Johannes has just given us an interesting explanation of the advantages and effects of drinking alcohol."

"Jeannette and I heard it," Tina said, "we were standing behind you, Uncle Nick."

"Do you agree with him?"

"I do not drink. But I think he spoke as a humanist."

"As a what?" Nick responded with apparent surprise. "This is a big word for me. Can you explain it in simple terms?"

"He spoke from a moral and rational point of view. He implies that human growth and development is the highest value in human life. A humanist stands on the ground of human values and does not deviate from them. They also believe that humanity is the highest dimension of being that God created!"

"These are bigger words, my dear!"

Tina was embarrassed, for she could not express her second explanation in simpler words. Nick noticed her reaction and decided not to press her for another explanation. Instead, he turned his attention to Johannes: "How is your work, Johannes. I hope you are making progress on your project!"

"Yes, I am. I plan to finish the first phase of my work at the end of next week. My next step is to travel to Damascus and then to Aleppo. These two cities will be centers from which I hope to branch out to the major historical sites of Syria. This phase will take about two to three months."

"Do you know what it is like to travel from one city to another in Syria?" Johannes stared at Nick with inquiring eyes. The question was simple and clear, but it was incomprehensible to Johannes.

"What Nick meant to tell you, Johannes," Jirji interceded, "is that traveling in Syria is not as simple as it is in Germany. You should draw a schedule of the sites you wish to visit, the time you plan to spend at each site, and the means of travel, and you should make arrangements for implementing this schedule, otherwise, you will lose a great deal of time and much of your focus on your work."

"What is even worse," Nick added, "is that, even though your visits to the different historical sites will be approved by the government, you will be under the vigilant eyes of some secret agents. They will treat you as a spy until they are absolutely certain that you are innocent! They may arrest you, they may ask you questions, they may torture you, and they may throw you in a dungeon until the end of time. I would be careful if I were you!"

"I fully agree with you, Nick," Yuri added, "he should protect himself against such possibilities as soon as possible."

"In fact, I think he is already being followed by some secret agents," Nadim said.

"I am certain that he is being followed by at least one secret agent," Yuri added, confirming Nick's fears. "The first thing you should do is go to the German Embassy in Damascus and inform them of the nature and purpose of your visit, and also of its duration. Then you should go to the Ministry of Education and secure legal permission from the Division of Cultural Affairs to visit the sites you need to visit. Finally, you need to hire a taxi driver to take you from one city to another and from one site to another."

"You have forgotten an important requirement, Yuri," Nick said.

"What is it?"

"Make sure that the taxi driver is an honest and legitimate driver."

"Yes," Yuri confirmed. "You see, most of the taxi drivers are secret agents, and most of the street cleaners, vendors, and beggars are also secret agents. We have been living in George Orwell's society years before he wrote his famous novel. We are the visionaries of the future of humanity!" Yuri made this remark with a cynical tinge in his voice! Johannes was astonished, indeed stunned, when he heard the comments made by Nick and Yuri. He did not expect to receive this kind of lesson about the country of his ancestors. A frown knotted his forehead, and he looked at Yuri and then at Nick with desperate eyes.

"It is clear that I shall need help!" Johannes mumbled. His face was exuding sadness and disappointment. Yuri understood Johannes's reaction. His heart ached for him. He also realized that it was essential for a man in his position to experience what it means to live in a developing country where people do not live in rationally founded institutions, in which a modicum of security, freedom, justice, and pleasure is a luxury.

"Please, dear Johannes," Yuri said, "I want you to refrain from worrying about your travel plans during your stay in Syria." That was the first time Yuri addressed Johannes as "dear." Tina and Johannes immediately noticed this change of attitude, and they felt the emotions that prompted Yuri to express himself in this way. They were pleased because they knew that Yuri was treating Johannes as family. "Tina and I," he continued, "will be going to Damascus a week from today. Tina has applied for a scholarship to do her graduate studies either in France or in England. We were hoping that if she passes the scholarship examination, she will attend either London University or the University of Paris. This examination will be given on the following Tuesday. I, too, shall have a meeting at the Ministry of Education.

"Armen, Tina, and I will go to Damascus next Sunday. You are welcome to accompany us on this trip. I shall be happy to take you to the German Embassy where you can report your visit to Syria and then to the Division of Cultural Affairs at the Ministry of Education, where you can obtain legal permission to visit the historical sites of your choice. You should present the documents you receive from the Embassy and the Ministry of Education at all hotels and historical sites, even museums, because many of the employees in these places are secret informants. Then we can visit the museum, the Damascus castle, and the old city of Damascus. The Omayyad Mosque, one of Syria's historical treasures, has witnessed the rise and fall of several civilizations during the past twenty centuries. What do you think of this proposal?"

"He does not need to think about it!" Nick was quick to say. Johannes shook his head and looked at Nick, then at Tina, and then at Yuri, an amazed expression painted his features.

"I am speechless, but—"

"No, buts!" Nick remarked.

"I fully agree with you, Uncle Nick!" Tina intervened. "It will be our pleasure to assist you and, more importantly, to be with you. Everyone in this family is fond of you." Neither Yuri nor any of the Mitya cousins, not even Jeannette, noticed the dampness that filled Johannes's eyes. Tina was happy, very happy! "They are tears of love, of our love," she thought.

"And the taxi driver?" Jirji exclaimed.

"I know the man you need for this job," Hanania volunteered. His name is Fadel Abdo. He is the father of my son's friend. He attends our church. I think he will agree to drive you to any corner of Syria."

"Who is touring Syria?" Deema, who just entered the living room, asked. She came to announce that dinner was served.

"Johannes." Nick tried to explain the nature of the tour to Deema as they were moving to the dining room.

Nick enjoyed family dinners immensely. He expressed his joy by welcoming his guests and family with a cheerful toast. That Sunday, his toast was directed at Johannes. "In these difficult times, we did not only receive the gift of a new Mitya member to the family but also the gift of good fortune. I propose a toast to our cousin, Johannes."

The proposal was followed by a wave of clicks and clacks. "I recommend the sfiha," Nick said to his new cousin, who happened to be sitting next to him. "It is my wife's specialty. No one can cook a better sfiha in the city of Latakia." But his wife was unable to appreciate the compliment of her husband, not because she did not deserve it or because she did not appreciate it, but because she was drowned in a puddle of sorrow for her daughter and the two young men in prison. "Have you come to a resolution about Faris's and Bassam's future? Will they hang Bassam? Will he rot in prison? And Faris? And—" She was going to wonder about Fadya's future, but she could not because her husband intervened.

"The man who can answer your questions in detail is Jirji. He has been talking with a lawyer about Faris's and Bassam's cases. He should give you an explanation of what we can expect. The picture is not as bleak as we had thought, my dear. Faris can get out of prison in a few months." A sigh of relief reverberated throughout the dining table. "As for Bassam, he will not be hanged. He may leave prison in a few years." Serene silence followed this short answer. It was broken by Deema.

"When will you be touring Syria, Johannes?" she asked.

"My tour will be a study tour. It is part of the research I am conducting on the remains of ancient Greek and Roman civilizations. Yuri, Nick, and Hanania were trying to determine the best way I can travel from one city to another."

"Will you be returning to Germany after you conclude your study?"

"Yes, in about two to three months."

"Do you mean that you will be returning to Germany for good? I was really hoping that Latakia was going to be your permanent home," Deema said with a touch of disappointment in her voice.

"I wish, but I teach there. My university expects me to resume my work next term." Deema fell silent, but not her eyes because they were fixed on Tina.

"We shall be losing you," Nick added, "and maybe Tina. No one knows how the world turns these days!"

"And Tina?" Jameela interjected with an unmistakable look of surprise. All eyes swarmed around Tina's face as if it hid some secret they wished to know.

"Tina will do her graduate study overseas— in London or Paris. She will be going to Damarcus to take a scholarship examination," and with a voice imbued with pride, Yuri added, "she will pass it with distinction the way she passed her exams here in Latakia."

"When do you plan to start your travels, Johannes?" Deema asked.

"Within two weeks."

Nadim's wife, who was overwhelmed by sadness over the imprisonment of her son, signaled to her husband that it was time for them to leave. They rose to their feet and bid Nick and Nora good-bye. "We hope to see you all at our house soon," Nadim said on his way out of the dining room. Yuri and his family followed them in a few minutes. Tina walked toward Johannes and whispered:

"We usually stroll on the cornice every Sunday afternoon. I will be delighted if you join us this Sunday."

"Your delight is my delight, my dear!"

"I shall be waiting for you."

"What time?"

"Five o'clock. I look forward with anticipation to seeing you then."

The Latakia cornice is usually crowded on Friday afternoon, the Muslim day of rest, and on Sunday afternoon, the Christian day of rest. It was crowded that afternoon. The azure sky stood as a dome over the blue Mediterranean, and the sun allowed its rays to dance leisurely over its ripples. It was a beautiful, mystical act of nature. Johannes felt a strong desire to contemplate that beauty and mystery. He expressed his wish to Tina. "Of course," she said, "I would very much like to share this experience with you, my dearest." They left Yuri and Armen and sat on a bench that faced the sea. They relished the beauty of the dancing rays on the ripples of the sea especially when the sun was setting behind the horizon and gradually transforming them into deep golden rays. The dance they watched was magnificent. They watched it for a while, and they felt the gentle breeze teasing their cheeks and their hearts. And yes, they expressed their tender feelings to one another and their desire to remain united forever and to grow from the flame of love in their hearts. To tell the truth, they were oblivious to the social environment surrounding them or the passage of time. On the contrary, time collapsed into a kind of eternal moment. Their parents came a few times to see if they were ready to go home, but they were reluctant to spoil the sanctity of their privacy.

Shortly after the sun abandoned the Latakia landscape, Tina said, "I would like you to come to our home tomorrow evening. I shall cook. Can you come?"

"Nothing gives more pleasure than to be with you. Believe me, if I tell you that I began to feel restless the moment my heart cried for you, and it cried for you the moment I saw you, not with my eyes but with my heart. A mysterious voice constantly whispers in my ears ever since that moment, 'You are alone; you should not be alone.' This voice does not only remind me of what I should do, but it also nags me when I fail to do what I should do. Yes, my dearest, I shall join you for supper tomorrow.' But, he added, "I have another idea."

"What is it?"

"I plan to finish the first phase of my work on Thursday evening. Instead of joining you tomorrow for supper, may we spend Friday together?" Tina did not answer him; she could not. Her eyes instantaneously gravitated toward his. They were tearing. She desired to embrace him, but she did not only because society frowned upon physical contact between men and women in public in those days. However, she was able to move closer to him and glide her hand slowly closer to his right side to touch his right hand, which was waiting for hers. Those two hands were locked in the warmest, tightest, and most intimate embrace, reflecting the desire of their hearts. They remained in that position until nature spread its dark cloak over the Latakia shore. Slow-moving footsteps awakened them from their sweetest reverie.

On the way to Bouqa that evening Jirji mentioned to Johannes that all the women in the family were convinced that he and Tina were interested in each other, "I noticed more than once that you paid special attention to her, but what I noticed was not a basis for a valid judgment. Is this true? Are you really interested in her—I mean romantically?"

"More than interested."

"What do you mean?"

"A few days ago, I felt that I was falling in love with her, but now I am absolutely certain that I am in love with her."

"Is she in love with you?"

"Yes, we are in love with one another. In fact, next Friday I shall spend the whole day with her and her parents, and I wish to spend as much time as I can with her. I do not know what will happen, but this is my innermost desire."

"That is wonderful news. I never thought that you would meet the love of your life here in Latakia. But you did. Deema, and I think the rest of the family would be happy to know that you and Tina are in love. I have a suspicion that Jeannette knows, but she guards Tina's secrets the way a hen guards her chicks. Deema was very sad when you mentioned this afternoon that you would return to Germany for good when you complete your research in Syria. This news will cheer her up. She believes, and I share her belief that you are the brightest presence in our lives. She has been dreading the moment of your departure. Your attachment, and hopefully your marriage, to Tina, will create a situation of active communication between us."

"Certainly. This evening we discussed the details of our trip to Damascus. During the discussion, we reflected on the plight which struck the

Mitya family. Yuri, Armen, and Tina expressed profound respect and love for you and Deema. You are dear to their hearts. I have a strong feeling that my visit to Latakia has created a firm bond between us."

"I share your feeling, Johannes. Let me bring to your attention some facts. In this society, young men and women shouldn't appear together in public if they are not engaged or married, otherwise, they will be the subject of malicious gossip. Such gossip can be harmful, especially to the woman. A ring on the finger silences such gossip.

"Next, if you feel inclined to get engaged, you will need a family by your side. Deema and I will be your family. Our customs and practices are complex. Most of them are historical relics, but it is wise not to rock the boat of culture at present. Finally, if you need any kind of help, you should feel free to let me know. You cannot afford to be bashful. I will be disappointed if you treat me as a stranger."

Johannes was speechless. He was overwhelmed by an explosion of emotions in his heart. When you are in the midst of such an explosion, the only meaningful language you can speak is the language of silence, the kind speaks without speaking. Johannes embraced Jirji's profile with a protracted gaze. Jirji felt it. He was in the presence of the sacred light of the human heart. Did he need to respond to it? Suppose he tried, what would, or could, he say? "Thank you" or some similar expression? How can such a response disclose the depth of the love he felt? Human language stands as an inadequate means of communication before this kind of light.

EIGHT

Tina and Johannes are Married

FRIDAY WAS A MAGICAL day for Tina and Johannes. They talked, flirted, laughed, and visited the landmarks of Latakia and its environs. The taxi was none other than that of Fadel, who Hanania had recommended. They even paid a short visit to Johannes's apartment in Bouqa. Tina stood before the papers and pamphlets that were spread on a rather large table for a few seconds and allowed a light smile to glide over her lips. "This is where he works," she thought. Frankly, she did not see papers and pamphlets; she saw ideas, she saw the living mind of her beloved! How can you remain silent or indifferent before this spectacle, one that many people cannot even notice, much less see? Tina moved closer toward Johannes and kissed him with all the passion she could muster. Her eyes did not tear, but they glistened a little. Johannes saw her eyes and felt their warmth. He could not kiss her back, only because he too was overwhelmed by emotion, but he embraced her with all his might. They walked to the door of the apartment in silence and then to the car.

Shortly after they were seated in the car, Johannes noted that Tina was thoughtful. He cast an inquiring glance at her, which she felt. "We should celebrate this day every month of our lives," she remarked.

"It is a good day, a memorable day. It will never die. It will thrive in my heart, and I hope yours forever!"

"It will thrive in one heart and one heart only: our heart." Johannes stretched his hand across the space between them and held her hand. The taxi driver was very discrete. He did not make any attempt to intrude into their privacy.

At noon the two lovers had lunch at Spiro's. The Mediterranean Sea stretched before their eyes like a sea of infinity. It was a beautiful scene, and it was a mystical moment. It was impossible for any aesthetically sensitive human being to overlook or ignore its beauty and mystery. Although their eyes were lost to it for several seconds, Johannes detected a shade of apprehension in Tina's eyes. He was perturbed. He could not remain indifferent to her feeling of apprehension, especially when he knew its cause. Was it the scholarship examination? Yes! He opened the subject and tried to reduce the sharp edge of her apprehension. He assured her more than once that she would excel in it. "You will always shine in whatever you do, my dearest," he emphasized. "It is normal to feel anxious when we take any kind of examination. I even think that a measure of anxiety accompanies any kind of creative activity. Ignorance of the outcome, even when we feel we have done well, is the source of the anxiety." Tina smiled, moved her hand across the table, and poured a load of love into it. He felt it.

It may seem strange to remark that when you truly love a woman, the way Johannes loved Tina, when you open up to her, when you feel attracted to her and allow yourself to be a voluntary captive to this attraction, when you delight in the fire that kindles in your heart, when you feel an irresistible desire to spend the rest of your life with her—yes, when you love her truly, and she loves you truly, you do not feel that you are a stranger to her, you do not need time to know her, to know her ways or even her habits, you do not need a period to adjust, and you do not need a shorter or longer time to trust her. Do you need to fulfill any of these conditions if you are an open book to her, if you are at home with her? Doesn't the love of your heart incline both of you to live from that very love? Isn't it a source of harmony? Don't the eyes of the heart, its ears, and its mind become the guide in whatever you do, think, and feel? What if you fulfill all these conditions, but your actions do not flow from that well of love, would your so-called love last?

Oh, how many people these days play the *game of love and loving*, to discover whether they are tailored for each other! Notice how they prepare lists of traits, habits, sexual desires or expectations or competencies, and other conditions when they meet or look for the love of their lives. They tend to forget that this someone is a human depth, a cry for human self-realization and that the language of this depth, and this cry, is quite different from the language of the social market of love!

Soon after he gave his last lesson on Saturday, Jirji went to Bouqa to fetch Johannes from his home. Deema and Jeannette were waiting for them. The afternoon was a family event. They reviewed Johannes's plans and expectations during the next two months, then they moved to the latest news about the elopement of Nick's daughter. Deema was surprised, Jirji gratified, and Johannes elated when Jeannette reported that Nick and his wife have reconciled with their daughter and that they were willing to accept her husband as a member of the family. "How did it happen?" Deema asked Jeannette.

"Uncle Nick initiated the process of reconciliation."

"Uncle Nick? Can it be?"

"Yes. No one knows why or how he had a radical change of heart. But Nora said that she began to notice a change of attitude toward his daughter after Faris was imprisoned and Jirji was already consulting with a lawyer about the cases of his nephews. Something happened during the past two weeks. "Not only his attitude toward his daughter and nephews has changed but also toward me and his life in general. It is like he is gradually becoming a new man—kinder, more respectful and more attentive to my needs and the needs of the children. I love this change, Jeannette!"

"I really hope, Deema, that the rest of the cousins learn the secret of being human from Uncle Jirji, Johannes, and now from Uncle Nick." She fell into a daze, and then, as trying to avoid this painful subject, she asked, "Have you seen the Sarkisians?" Deema asked, changing the topic of their conversation.

"Yes, this morning. Armen and Tina were doing some shopping. They are looking forward to their trip to Damascus tomorrow. Jeannette threw a teasing smile at Johannes and said, "What have you done to Tina?"

"What do you mean?"

"You should know what I mean. You must be a magician! Yes, you are one! You know how a woman thinks, desires, and feels. Where did you learn this skill?"

"Skill?"

"Yes!"

"If it is a skill, ask my heart. She and no one else can answer your question!"

"I do not think it is a skill. It must be magic. You must have transported her to the seventh heaven. I have never encountered a woman in love like Tina in my life! Many, if not all, of the men in Latakia, should learn the art of charming a woman from you." Johannes blushed when he heard those words.

"The reverse of what you said, Jeannette, is the truth. It is she who charmed me. She is the charmer, not I. Yes, I am charmed by her beauty, intellectual excellence, and purity of heart. But these qualities, viewed singly or collectively, are not the source of her charm. These qualities and something more, something mystical, something indefinable, something divine about her, within her that transmits this charm. Even the gods would be captivated by this kind of charm!"

"I have a gut feeling, Johannes, that your love for one another was fashioned by the hands of Aphrodite and no other hands! No one can blame you for acting and feeling the way you do."

"Are you sure?"

"Yes," and changing the subject, Jeannette asked, "you will be returning to Germany in two or three months. I cannot imagine you and Tina living apart from each other. Have you thought about what will happen when, or before, you leave for Germany?"

"Yes. To tell the truth, I have not stopped thinking about this question ever since my heart was entwined with hers. I think it is wise to wait until she writes her scholarship examination."

"But if she receives a government scholarship, she will be doing her graduate work either in London or Paris. And she will be obliged to teach at a Syrian institution of higher learning."

"I am aware of this fact. But there are other options. Tina and I will discuss them and choose one." He paused thoughtfully for a moment and continued, "My dear Jeannette, I cannot live without Tina. I prefer to lose myself than lose her, and I prefer to be away from myself than be away from her."

Love continued to blossom in Tina's and Johannes's hearts. One month after Johannes began his visits to the historical sites in the Damascus district, they were formally engaged. Jirji stood at Johannes's right side, and Nick was on his left hand; Deema stood on Tina's right hand and Jeannette on her left hand. Yuri and Armen stood next to them as their guardian angels throughout the engagement ceremony. They blessed their daughter and future son-in-law with a smile of their love and approval. Everyone in the family and some friends and neighbors attended the ceremony. It was simple but beautiful. The lovers were allowed to kiss on the lips after the priest blessed them with his holy cross.

It became clear to Tina, her parents, and the whole family that she would do her graduate work at the University of Hamburg. Johannes assured her that, given her credentials and especially the fact that she passed the scholarship examination with distinction, she would receive a graduate scholarship from the department of political science, and she did.

On Christmas day of that year, Johannes and Tina were married. The wedding was attended by Tina's parents, Jeannette, Jirji and Deema, Nick and Nora, Hanania and Jameela, and me, the writer of the history of this slice in the life of the Mitya family. Abraham and his mother boycotted not only the engagement and wedding ceremonies but also any news about the newly established Mitya family in Germany. Nadim could not attend the wedding because he was heavily involved in the legal proceedings of his son's case.

Although I was able to attend the wedding in Germany, I could not linger there for a long time. During the past few months, I heard that, in the following few years, Tina received a doctorate degree in political science and started in-depth research about the history of the Middle East. I also heard that the university awarded Johannes a professorship based on the research he did in Syria. Tina and Johannes had one child, a daughter, when I wrote these lines. Yuri and Armen, along with Jirji and Deema, visited Tina and Johannes many times after they were married. I was also informed that on one of her visits to Tina in Germany, Jeannette met a German engineer whom she married six months later. Her father, Abraham, was furious when she asked for his approval; he declined her request. But she rebelled against her father and traveled to Germany against his wishes. Jirji, Nadim, and Nick and their wives stood with her against Abraham. They took charge of all her expenses and stood next to her at the wedding ceremony. Jeannette and her husband live in a house close to Tina's and Johannes's home. As far as I know, both families are leading happy lives!

You may wonder, dear reader, why I have not recounted any details about the lives of the Mitya family in Germany. The reason is simple. I cannot write about anything unless I have personally experienced it, otherwise, my writing would be based on hearsay, but hearsay is not a reliable source of true information. It can never be. It can sometimes be useful, but it can never be a source of indubitable truth. I prize honesty more than anything in this world. Happiness and human progress, in general, are not possible if the beliefs and the values we seek to realize in our lives are not founded in the truth of what we experience. Writing based on hearsay is an insult to human dignity. Unfortunately, much of what we read nowadays in philosophy, literature, and the news media does not arise from the bosom of human experience, from the truth of the struggle of human beings for perfection, but from a desire to produce some kind of temporary advantage or pleasure. I shy away from this kind of writing.